飞鸟集·吉檀迦利
泰戈尔诗选新译

STRAY BIRDS
GITANJALI

Rabindranath
Tagore

(印)泰戈尔/著
黄华勇/译

图书在版编目（CIP）数据

飞鸟集·吉檀迦利：泰戈尔诗选新译 /(印) 泰戈尔著；黄华勇译. —北京：中国书籍出版社，2021.2
ISBN 978-7-5068-5912-7

Ⅰ.①飞… Ⅱ.①泰… ②黄… Ⅲ.①诗集—印度—现代 Ⅳ.①I351.25

中国版本图书馆CIP数据核字（2021）第038832号

飞鸟集·吉檀迦利：泰戈尔诗选新译

(印) 泰戈尔著；黄华勇译

责任编辑	王星舒　王　淼
责任印制	孙马飞　马　芝
封面设计	中尚图
出版发行	中国书籍出版社
地　　址	北京市丰台区三路居路 97 号（邮编：100073）
电　　话	（010）52257143（总编室）（010）52257140（发行部）
电子邮箱	eo@chinabp.com.cn
经　　销	全国新华书店
印　　刷	天宇万达印刷有限公司
开　　本	880 毫米×1230 毫米　1/32
字　　数	174千字
印　　张	10
版　　次	2021年4月第1版　2021年4月第1次印刷
书　　号	ISBN 978-7-5068-5912-7
定　　价	68.00 元

版权所有　翻印必究

译者自序

泰戈尔是在东西方均享有盛誉的大诗人,《吉檀迦利》和《飞鸟集》乃经久不衰的传世名作,都入选了我国教育部推荐中学生课外阅读书目,无须过多介绍。两作均有多种译本,尤以冰心先生的《吉檀迦利》译本和郑振铎先生的《飞鸟集》译本流传最广、影响最深。冰心先生和郑振铎先生都是文坛巨擘,一代宗师,在白话文学史上开风气之先,自不待说,其余如白开元先生、徐翰林先生等,也都是学养深厚的大家。既然如此,《吉檀迦利》和《飞鸟集》还有新译的必要吗?这也是我第一次读到《飞鸟集》新译本时的疑问。

2015年12月22日,我偶然在网上看到一篇文章,说冯唐先生翻译的《飞鸟集》因翻译风格和个别用词的问题引起轩然大波。我的第一感觉是《飞鸟集》已有郑振铎先生的经典译本,按说,后来者应该如李白登临黄鹤楼一样,只能发出"眼前有景道不得,崔颢题诗在上头"的感叹。写作方面,冯唐先生是行家,既然他要重译《飞鸟集》,自有他的道理。为解开疑惑,我找来郑振铎先生翻译的《飞鸟集》重新阅读。读了一部分之后,也觉得《飞鸟集》确实还有再译的空间,但这种空间的存在，不是因为郑振铎先生的水平不够，而是时代的原因使然，当时的白话文还不够圆熟。我一时兴起，便译了十余首发表在微信公众号。

如第 10 首：
Sorrow is hushed into peace in my heart like the evening among the silent trees.

忧伤平复于我心，如夜幕消融于幽林。

第 176 首：
The water in a vessel is sparkling; the water in the sea is dark.

The small truth has words that are clear; the great truth has great silence.

杯水透亮，海水幽暗。

小道行文，大道不言。

第 283 首：
While I was passing with the crowd in the road I saw thy smile from the balcony and I sang and forgot all noise.

当我随着路上拥挤的人潮，望见你在阳台上嫣然一笑，我唱起歌，忘了所有喧嚣。

第 323 首：

I have suffered and despaired and known death and I am glad that I am in this great world.

我受过苦难，有过绝望，尝过死亡，但庆幸我依然活在这伟大的世上。

一些朋友读了之后，问我是否能把《飞鸟集》通译出来。那段时间，我辞职出来，在北京折腾一点事情，时间相对自由，便斗胆尝试。时隔多年，当我经历了一些事情后，再读《飞鸟集》英文版，生发出很多以前体会不到的感受。恰如蒋捷的《虞美人·听雨》所言："少年听雨歌楼上，红烛昏罗帐。壮年听雨客舟中，江阔云低，断雁叫西风。"因此，我把翻译当作一次精读，一次与泰戈尔的久别重逢，用了近三个月的时间完成《飞鸟集》的译文初稿，此后陆续修改，到 2020 年 12 月 8 日交稿，历时五年方才定稿。

在翻译《飞鸟集》的过程中，我又找来泰戈尔其他的诗作阅读。读完《吉檀迦利》的第一首，我就深感震撼，若说《飞鸟集》是一条溪流，《吉檀迦利》则是一片汪洋。《吉檀迦利》是 Gitanjali 的音译，意为献歌，是献给神的诗歌。诗作大多以 I（我）对 Thou（You，你）诉说的形式展开，

Thou 是 God（神），对于有宗教信仰者，可以把自己所信仰的神代入，对于没有宗教信仰者，可把神当作一个远古的智者，一个睿智的长辈，一个知心的朋友，或是心灵深处的另一个自己，每一首诗都像静夜的一次促膝长谈。因此，从2018年初开始，我着手翻译《吉檀迦利》，用了半年时间完成初稿，历时三年定稿。

在接洽出版事宜之初，编辑曾问我此前是否有中英文的学习或创作经历，我坦言没有。1984 年，我出生于湖南郴州一个叫大山口的小山村，从村名就可以想见那里是何等的荒僻。母亲不识字，父亲读过高中，但常年在外，小时候家里没有什么书可读。大概上小学四年级时，父亲带回一本《唐祝文周四才子传》。这本书算不上高明的文学作品，反而有点恶趣味，但四大才子经常游戏笔墨，玩一些对联、小令等文字游戏，让我知道了文字的妙趣，那本书几乎被我翻烂了。考到郴州市二中念高中之后，我才有机会读到大量的文学作品。那时，学校附近有一家卖盗版书的小书店，花六七块钱就能买到一本世界名著，如《巴黎圣母院》《复活》《简爱》《三个火枪手》，我每月都会买几本。从那家店里，还买到一本《金圣叹评点才子古文》，二十多年来，我辗转多地，曾在郴州、天津、厦门、佛山、北京等多个城市生活，其间丢失了很多书，但这本我一直带在身边，至今未丢失。2004年，我考入南开大学，学的是人力资源管理专业，旁听过几节中文系的课，但更多的时间，还是流连于学校附近的旧书市场。在文学方面，我可说是没有师承。如果一定要找师承，我的老师便是老子、屈原、庄子、司马迁、陶渊明、李白、杜甫、苏东坡、兰陵笑笑生、曹雪芹、鲁迅、沈从文、穆旦、王道乾、余光中、莎士比亚、雨果、托尔斯泰、泰戈尔、陀思妥耶夫斯基等中外先贤。每一次阅读他们的不朽作品，都能穿越时空，聆听他们的教诲，感受他们的伟大心灵。只是因为我自己愚钝，他们是大海，我所学到的只是一滴水。即便如此，有心的读者应该可以在我的译文里，看见他们的身影。

希望这个新译本，给读过《飞鸟集》和《吉檀迦利》的读者带来一些新的感悟，让第一次阅读《飞鸟集》和《吉檀迦利》的读者，对泰戈尔的诗作留下美好的印象和重读的欲望。译文难免有错误和疏漏之处，还请读者见谅，并不吝指正。

黄华勇
2021 年 2 月 22 日于郴州

目 录
Contents

飞鸟集
001

吉檀迦利
167

飞鸟集
Stray Birds

1

Stray birds of summer come to my window to sing and fly away.

And yellow leaves of autumn, which have no songs, flutter and fall there with a sigh.

夏日悠闲的鸟儿来到我的窗前,唱着歌,又飞走了。
而秋天的黄叶没有歌唱,叹息一声,飘落在那里。

2

O Troupe of little vagrants of the world, leave your footprints in my words.

那一小队浪迹天涯的卖艺人,请把你们的足迹,留在我的诗文里。

3

The world puts off its mask of vastness to its lover.
It becomes small as one song, as one kiss of the eternal.

世界对着它的爱人揭下浩瀚的面纱。
它变得微小,如一曲轻歌,如一个永恒之吻。

4

It is the tears of the earth that keep her smiles in bloom.

是大地的泪水,使她的笑颜绽放。

5

The mighty desert is burning for the love of a blade of grass who shakes her head and laughs and flies away.

大漠如火,热恋草叶,芳草摇头,一笑而去。

6

If you shed tears when you miss the sun, you also miss the stars.

如果你因为错失太阳而垂泪,你亦将错过星辰。

7

The sands in your way beg for your song and your movement, dancing water. Will you carry the burden of their lameness?

欢舞的流水,你途中的泥沙乞求你的歌唱、你的律动。你愿背负这残缺的累赘前行吗?

8

Her wishful face haunts my dreams like the rain at night.

她热切的容颜,如夜雨萦绕我的梦魂。

9

Once we dreamt that we were strangers.

We wake up to find that we were dear to each other.

曾经梦见我们形同陌路。

醒来方觉我们彼此相依。

10

Sorrow is hushed into peace in my heart like the evening among the silent trees.

忧伤平复于我心,如夜幕消融于幽林。

11

Some unseen fingers, like an idle breeze, are playing upon my heart the music of the ripples.

无形之手，忽如轻风，拨我心弦，泛起涟漪。

12

"What language is thine, O sea?"
"The language of eternal question."
"What language is thy answer, O sky?"
"The language of eternal silence."

"大海，你有何言？"
"永恒的追问。"
"苍天，你以何答？"
"亘古的沉默。"

13

Listen, my heart, to the whispers of the world with which it makes love to you.

我的心，听那世界的呢喃，那是对你的示爱。

14

The mystery of creation is like the darkness of night—it is great. Delusions of knowledge are like the fog of the morning.

造物之玄妙，如暗夜之恢弘。格物之虚幻，如晨雾之缥缈。

15

Do not seat your love upon a precipice because it is high.

勿因仰慕峭壁之高，便以爱情攀附其上。

16

I sit at my window this morning where the world like a passer-by stops for a moment, nods to me and goes.

清晨我坐在窗前，世界像一个过客，停下脚步朝我点点头，便离去了。

17

These little thoughts are the rustle of leaves; they have their whisper of joy in my mind.

这些细微的思绪如树叶的窸窣,在我心中欢快地私语。

18

What you are you do not see, what you see is your shadow.

真我不可见,所见乃幻影。

19

My wishes are fools, they shout across thy song, my Master.
Let me but listen.

主啊，我的祈求如此愚妄，喧嚣着扰乱你的圣歌。
让我只是聆听。

20

I cannot choose the best.
The best chooses me.

我不能选择最好的。
而是最好的选择我。

21

They throw their shadows before them who carry their lantern on their back.

负明灯于背后者，投暗影于身前。

22

That I exist is a perpetual surprise which is life.

我的存在是一个无尽的奇迹，这便是生命。

23

"We, the rustling leaves, have a voice that answers the storms, but who are you so silent?"

"I am a mere flower."

"我们这萧萧的树叶都有声音回应风雨,而你是谁,竟如此沉默?"

"我只是一朵花。"

24

Rest belongs to the work as the eyelids to the eyes.

休息之于劳作,如眼睑之于眼睛。

25

Man is a born child, his power is the power of growth.

人是初生之子,他的力量是生长的力量。

26

God expects answers for the flowers he sends us, not for the sun and the earth.

神期望我们回应的,是他馈赠我们的花朵,而非太阳和土地。

27

The light that plays, like a naked child, among the green leaves happily knows not that man can lie.

光束如赤裸的孩子,在绿叶丛中尽情嬉闹,不知世间还有谎言。

28

O Beauty, find thyself in love, not in the flattery of thy mirror.

美啊,从爱中寻找真我,而不是从镜子的谄媚里寻找。

29

My heart beats her waves at the shore of the world and writes upon it her signature in tears with the words, "I love thee."

我的心以她的浪花激荡着世界的海岸,用泪水在边上写下印记:"我爱你。"

30

"Moon, for what do you wait?"
"To salute the sun for whom I must make way."

"月亮,你在等待什么?"
"向我必须让路的太阳致敬。"

31

The trees come up to my window like the yearning voice of the dumb earth.

绿树探身到我窗前,如沉默大地渴望的呼唤。

32

His own mornings are new surprises to God.

神自己的清晨,也都是新的惊喜。

33

Life finds its wealth by the claims of the world, and its worth by the claims of love.

生命通过世间的需求获取财富,通过爱的需求实现价值。

34

The dry river-bed finds no thanks for its past.

枯竭的河床毫不感念它的过往。

35

The bird wishes it were a cloud. The cloud wishes it were a bird.

鸟愿化作一朵云,云想变成一只鸟。

36

The waterfall sings, "I find my song, when I find my freedom."

瀑布唱道:"我找到自由就找到了歌声。"

37

I cannot tell why this heart languishes in silence.

It is for small needs it never asks, or knows or remembers.

我说不清这颗心为何在沉寂中颓丧。

为了那未曾索要、未曾了解、未曾记取的小小欲求。

38

Woman, when you move about in your household service your limbs sing like a hill stream among its pebbles.

姑娘,当你料理家务时,你的手足歌唱,如山泉流过卵石。

39

The sun goes to cross the Western sea, leaving its last salutation to the East.

太阳越过西方的大海,向东方致以最后的敬礼。

40

Do not blame your food because you have no appetite.

勿因没有食欲而责怪食物。

41

The trees, like the longings of the earth, stand a-tiptoe to peep at the heaven.

树丛如大地的渴望，踮着脚向长空窥探。

42

You smiled and talked to me of nothing and I felt that for this I had been waiting long.

你微笑着，什么都没说，我感到为了这一刻我已等了很久。

43

The fish in the water is silent, the animal on the earth is noisy, the bird in the air is singing,

But Man has in him the silence of the sea, the noise of the earth and the music of the air.

水里的游鱼沉静,地上的走兽喧闹,空中的飞鸟歌唱;
而人类兼具大海的沉静,大地的喧闹,天空的音乐。

44

The world rushes on over the strings of the lingering heart making the music of sadness.

世界从彷徨的心弦上掠过,奏出忧郁的乐章。

45

He has made his weapons his gods. When his weapons win he is defeated himself.

他奉剑为神,剑胜而身败。

46

God finds himself by creating.

神以创造发现自我。

47

Shadow, with her veil drawn, follows Light in secret meekness, with her silent steps of love.

影子蒙着面纱,用无声的爱的脚步,悄悄地、温柔地尾随着光。

48

The stars are not afraid to appear like fireflies.

群星不在乎看起来像萤火。

49

I thank thee that I am none of the wheels of power but I am one with the living creatures that are crushed by it.

感谢你,我不是强权的轮子,而是强权轮子碾压下的生灵之一。

50

The mind, sharp but not broad, sticks at every point but does not move.

心念敏锐而不博大,执着而不融通。

51

Your idol is shattered in the dust to prove that God's dust is greater than your idol.

你的偶像消散在尘埃中，证明神的尘埃比你的偶像更伟大。

52

Man does not reveal himself in his history, he struggles up through it.

人不能在他的历史中彰显自己，而是从中奋起。

53

While the glass lamp rebukes the earthen for calling it cousin, the moon rises, and the glass lamp, with a bland smile, calls her, "My dear, dear sister."

琉璃灯因陶灯叫它表兄而生气。当明月升起,琉璃灯笑脸相迎:"我亲爱的,亲爱的姐姐。"

54

Like the meeting of the seagulls and the waves we meet and come near. The seagulls fly off, the waves roll away and we depart.

如海鸥邂逅波涛,我们相逢、靠近。海鸥高飞,波涛远去,我们分离。

55

My day is done, and I am like a boat drawn on the beach, listening to the dance-music of the tide in the evening.

白昼已尽,我如岸边疲倦的小船,聆听着晚潮的舞曲。

56

Life is given to us, we earn it by giving it.

天赋生命,唯有奉献,方可得到。

57

We come nearest to the great when we are great in humility.

我们极度谦卑时,最接近伟大。

58

The sparrow is sorry for the peacock at the burden of its tail.

麻雀为孔雀背负尾翎而担忧。

59

Never be afraid of the moments—thus sings the voice of the everlasting.

永远不要害怕刹那——永恒之声如此歌唱。

60

The hurricane seeks the shortest road by the no-road, and suddenly ends its search in the Nowhere.

飓风在无路中寻找最短之路，突然在虚无之境终止了它的追寻。

61

Take my wine in my own cup, friend.

It loses its wreath of foam when poured into that of others.

请用我的杯饮我的酒,朋友。

若倒入他人杯中,它会失去欢腾的泡沫。

62

The Perfect decks itself in beauty for the love of the Imperfect.

完美为了对不完美的爱,把自己打扮得美丽。

63

God says to man, "I heal you therefore I hurt, love you therefore punish."

神对人说:"我治愈你所以伤害你,爱你所以惩戒你。"

64

Thank the flame for its light, but do not forget the lampholder standing in the shade with constancy of patience.

感谢灯火的光明,但别忘了坚忍伫立于暗影中的掌灯人。

65

Tiny grass, your steps are small, but you possess the earth under your tread.

小草,你的步履虽小,但拥有你走过的土地。

66

The infant flower opens its bud and cries, "Dear World, please do not fade."

娇嫩的花儿张开它的花蕾呼喊:"亲爱的世界,请不要凋零。"

67

God grows weary of great kingdoms, but never of little flowers.

上帝会厌弃伟大的帝国,但永不遗忘微小的花朵。

68

Wrong cannot afford defeat but Right can.

谬误经不起失败,但真理无所畏惧。

69

"I give my whole water in joy," sings the waterfall, "though little of it is enough for the thirsty."

瀑布唱道:"我愿欣然倾尽所有,虽然口渴者只需一瓢。"

70

Where is the fountain that throws up these flowers in a ceaseless outbreak of ecstasy?

鲜花如泉涌,怒放无止境,其源头何在?

71

The woodcutter's axe begged for its handle from the tree.
The tree gave it.

樵夫之斧向树索要木柄。
树给了它。

72

In my solitude of heart I feel the sigh of this widowed evening veiled with mist and rain.

在我孤寂的心中,我感到黄昏如嫠妇,在雨雾的面纱下叹息。

73

Chastity is a wealth that comes from abundance of love.

忠贞是大爱的馈赠。

74

The mist, like love, plays upon the heart of the hills and brings out surprises of beauty.

迷雾如爱情,嬉戏于峰峦的心头,幻化出惊艳之美。

75

We read the world wrong and say that it deceives us.

我们误解了世界,却说世界欺骗了我们。

76

The poet wind is out over the sea and the forest to seek his own voice.

诗情如风,穿越大海和森林,去追寻自己的声音。

77

Every child comes with the message that God is not yet discouraged of man.

每一个新生儿,都带着神没有对人类失望的讯息。

78

The grass seeks her crowd in the earth.
The tree seeks his solitude of the sky.

小草在大地寻找她的同伴,
大树向长空追寻他的孤独。

79

Man barricades against himself.

人常常对自己设置障碍。

80

Your voice, my friend, wanders in my heart, like the muffled sound of the sea among these listening pines.

朋友，你的声音回荡在我心中，如低沉的海风穿过那倾听的松林。

81

What is this unseen flame of darkness whose sparks are the stars?

这不见火焰的黑暗,以繁星为火花,究竟是什么?

82

Let life be beautiful like summer flowers and death like autumn leaves.

使生命灿若夏花,死亡美如秋叶。

83

He who wants to do good knocks at the gate; he who loves finds the gate open.

欲行善者在门口敲门,爱人者发现门已敞开。

84

In death the many becomes one; in life the one becomes many. Religion will be one when God is dead.

死,万物化一;生,一生万物。
神若死亡,众教归一。

85

The artist is the lover of Nature, therefore he is her slave and her master.

艺术家是大自然的情人,所以他既为其仆,又为其主。

86

"How far are you from me, O Fruit?"
"I am hidden in your heart, O Flower."

"果实啊,你离我多远?"
"花儿呀,我藏于你心。"

87

This longing is for the one who is felt in the dark, but not seen in the day.

这份期盼,是为了那个在夜里触手可及,在白天却不见踪影的人。

88

"You are the big drop of dew under the lotus leaf, I am the smaller one on its upper side," said the dewdrop to the lake.

露珠对湖水说:"你是荷叶下的大露珠,我是荷叶上的小露珠。"

89

The scabbard is content to be dull when it protects the keenness of the sword.

为保护剑的锋利，剑鞘甘愿迟钝。

90

In darkness the One appears as uniform; in the light the One appears as manifold.

黑暗中万物同一，光明中一化万象。

91

The great earth makes herself hospitable with the help of the grass.

苍茫大地因芳草而变得妩媚动人。

92

The birth and death of the leaves are the rapid whirls of the eddy whose wider circles move slowly among stars.

树叶的生与死是旋涡的急速飞旋,而旋涡广袤的边缘在星斗间缓缓移动。

93

Power said to the world, "You are mine."
The world kept it prisoner on her throne.
Love said to the world, "I am thine."
The world gave it the freedom of her house.

强权正告世界:"你属于我。"
世界将其囚禁于王座。
爱情告诉世界:"我归于你。"
世界赋她自由的家园。

94

The mist is like the earth's desire. It hides the sun for whom she cries.

雾霭如大地的渴望,遮蔽了她所呼唤的太阳。

95

Be still, my heart, these great trees are prayers.

平静吧,我的心,这些大树都是祈祷者。

96

The noise of the moment scoffs at the music of the Eternal.

片刻的喧嚣嘲笑着永恒的乐章。

97

I think of other ages that floated upon the stream of life and love and death and are forgotten, and I feel the freedom of passing away.

我想起那些时代,漂浮在生、死与爱的长河上,想到这一切终被遗忘,便感到离世而去的释然。

98

The sadness of my soul is her bride's veil.
It waits to be lifted in the night.

我灵魂深处的忧伤,像新娘的面纱,等着在夜里被撩起。

99

Death's stamp gives value to the coin of life; making it possible to buy with life what is truly precious.

死亡的印鉴给人生的货币赋值，使其能以生命购买真正的宝物。

100

The cloud stood humbly in a corner of the sky.
The morning crowned it with splendour.

云朵谦逊地站在天边，晨曦为它戴上壮丽的冠冕。

101

The dust receives insult and in return offers her flowers.

尘土受辱,报以花朵。

102

Do not linger to gather flowers to keep them, but walk on, for flowers will keep themselves blooming all your way.

不要停下来采集花朵,一路前行,花儿自会在你的路上盛开。

103

Roots are the branches down in the earth.

Branches are roots in the air.

根是地下的枝。

枝是空中的根。

104

The music of the far-away summer flutters around the Autumn seeking its former nest.

夏日已然远去，余音在秋天徘徊，寻觅着它的旧巢。

105

Do not insult your friend by lending him merits from your own pocket.

不要把你口袋里的勋章借给你的朋友来侮辱他。

106

The touch of the nameless days clings to my heart like mosses round the old tree.

无名日子的感触,缠绕在我心头,如苔藓爬满了老树。

107

The echo mocks her origin to prove she is the original.

回声嘲笑原声,以证明她是原声。

108

God is ashamed when the prosperous boasts of His special favour.

当富人夸耀他得到的眷顾,上帝感到羞愧。

109

I cast my own shadow upon my path, because I have a lamp that has not been lighted.

我的身影投在路上,因为我还有一盏灯没有点亮。

110

Man goes into the noisy crowd to drown his own clamour of silence.

人走进喧嚣的人群,以掩盖他无声的呐喊。

111

That which ends in exhaustion is death, but the perfect ending is in the endless.

死亡止于枯竭,圆满终于无穷。

112

The sun has his simple robe of light. The clouds are decked with gorgeousness.

太阳只穿着朴素的光裳,云彩却打扮得金碧辉煌。

113

The hills are like shouts of children who raise their arms, trying to catch stars.

群峰如欢呼的孩童,举起手臂试图摘取星星。

114

The road is lonely in its crowd for it is not loved.

熙攘的道路是孤独的,因为没有人爱它。

115

The power that boasts of its mischiefs is laughed at by the yellow leaves that fall, and clouds that pass by.

强权夸耀它的恶行,飘零的黄叶和悠然的浮云笑了。

116

The earth hums to me to-day in the sun, like a woman at her spining, some ballad of the ancient time in a forgotten tongue.

今天,大地在阳光下对我轻唱,像一个织布的妇人,用被遗忘的语言,哼着古老的歌谣。

117

The grass-blade is worthy of the great world where it grows.

寸草无愧于他生长的伟大世界。

118

Dream is a wife who must talk.
Sleep is a husband who silently suffers.

梦是一个喋喋不休的妻子，
睡是一个默默忍耐的丈夫。

119

The night kisses the fading day whispering to his ear, "I am death, your mother. I am to give you fresh birth."

黑夜与白昼吻别,在他耳边低语:"我是死亡,你的母亲,我将给你新生。"

120

I feel, thy beauty, dark night, like that of the loved woman when she has put out the lamp.

黑夜,我感觉,你的美恰如一位佳人在她熄灭灯光的那一刻。

121

I carry in my world that flourishes the worlds that have failed.

我把逝去世界的繁华带到我的世界里。

122

Dear friend, I feel the silence of your great thoughts of many a deepening eventide on this beach when I listen to these waves.

亲爱的朋友，多少深沉的黄昏，当我在海边聆听涛声，便感知到你伟大思想的寂寥。

123

The bird thinks it is an act of kindness to give the fish a lift in the air.

鸟儿认为把鱼带到空中是善举。

124

"In the moon thou sendest thy love letters to me," said the night to the sun.

"I leave my answers in tears upon the grass."

夜晚对太阳说:"在明月里,你把情书寄给我。"
"我把回信留在了草叶的泪珠里。"

125

The great is a born child; when he dies he gives his great childhood to the world.

伟人是新生之子,当他死去,他把伟大的童年留给世界。

126

Not hammer strokes, but dance of the water sings the pebbles into perfection.

不是棒槌的击打,而是流水的轻歌曼舞,让鹅卵石臻于完美。

127

Bees sip honey from flowers and hum their thanks when they leave.

The gaudy butterfly is sure that the flowers owe thanks to him.

蜜蜂从花中采蜜,临走时嗡嗡地致以谢意。

而花蝴蝶确信是花儿欠它一份情意。

128

To be outspoken is easy when you do not wait to speak the complete truth.

如果不必说出全部的事实,畅所欲言并非难事。

129

Asks the Possible to the Impossible, "Where is your dwelling place?"

"In the dreams of the impotent," comes the answer.

"可能"问"不可能":"你栖身何处?"
它答道:"我在无能者的梦里。"

130

If you shut your door to all errors truth will be shut out.

若你将所有错误拒之门外,真理也不得而入。

∽ 131 ∾

I hear some rustle of things behind my sadness of heart, —I cannot see them.

我听见一些事物在我心中的忧伤后窸窣作响,却看不见它们。

∽ 132 ∾

Leisure in its activity is work.
The stillness of the sea stirs in waves.

忙里偷闲也是工作,
平静大海孕育风波。

133

The leaf becomes flower when it loves.
The flower becomes fruit when it worships.

叶子恋爱时开花。
花儿礼拜时结果。

134

The roots below the earth claim no rewards for making the branches fruitful.

地下的树根,让果实挂满枝头,却不求回报。

135

This rainy evening the wind is restless.

I look at the swaying branches and ponder over the greatness of all things.

如此雨夜,风吹不息。
观木叶之摇落,念万物之伟大。

136

Storm of midnight, like a giant child awakened in the untimely dark, has begun to play and shout.

子夜的风暴像一个巨婴,在不合时宜的黑暗中醒来并开始嬉闹。

137

Thou raisest thy waves vainly to follow thy lover. O sea, thou lonely bride of the storm.

大海,你这孤寂的暴风雨的新娘,徒劳地掀起巨浪追赶你的情郎。

138

"I am ashamed of my emptiness," said the Word to the Work.

"I know how poor I am when I see you," said the Work to the Word.

文章对功业说:"我为我的空洞感到惭愧。"

功业对文章说:"我看到你,才知道自己多么贫乏。"

139

Time is the wealth of change, but the clock in its parody makes it mere change and no wealth.

时间是流转的财富,但钟表只能模仿时间流逝,而不能创造财富。

140

Truth in her dress finds facts too tight.
In fiction she moves with ease.

真理在事实的装束里感到局促,在想象中行动自如。

141

When I travelled to here and to there, I was tired of thee, O Road, but now when thou leadest me to everywhere I am wedded to thee in love.

路啊，以前四处奔波时，我厌倦你。但现在，你引领我到每个地方，我就爱上你，想与你厮守终生。

142

Let me think that there is one among those stars that guides my life through the dark unknown.

我想，在满天繁星中，有一颗能指引我的人生穿越那未知的黑暗。

143

Woman, with the grace of your fingers you touched my things and order came out like music.

姑娘,当你用优雅的手指触碰我的物品,秩序便如音乐一样涌出。

144

One sad voice has its nest among the ruins of the years.
It sings to me in the night,—"I loved you."

一个悲伤的声音在时光的废墟里筑巢。
它在夜晚对我轻唱:"我爱你。"

145

The flaming fire warns me off by its own glow.

Save me from the dying embers hidden under ashes.

燃烧的火焰用它的光热警告我离开。

将我从隐藏在灰烬里的余火中救出来。

146

I have my stars in the sky,

But oh for my little lamp unlit in my house.

我有满天繁星,

却无斗室灯火。

147

The dust of the dead words clings to thee.
Wash thy soul with silence.

死寂语言的尘埃沾染你,
请用静默拂拭你的灵魂。

148

Gaps are left in life through which comes the sad music of death.

生命留下裂缝,从中传来死亡的悲歌。

149

The world has opened its heart of light in the morning.
Come out, my heart, with thy love to meet it.

世界在清晨敞开了光明之心。
出来吧,我的心,带着你的爱去迎接它。

150

My thoughts shimmer with these shimmering leaves and my heart sings with the touch of this sunlight; my life is glad to be floating with all things into the blue of space, into the dark of time.

我的思绪随着闪烁的树叶闪烁,我的心在阳光的轻抚下歌唱;我的生命随着万物欢快地漂浮在空间的蔚蓝里,在时间的幽暗中。

151

God's great power is in the gentle breeze, not in the storm.

神的伟大力量，在和风中，而非风暴里。

152

This is a dream in which things are all loose and they oppress. I shall find them gathered in thee when I awake and shall be free.

这是一场梦，梦中的一切都散开并压迫着我。当我醒来，发现它们都聚集在你那里，我又轻松了。

153

"Who is there to take up my duties?" asked the setting sun.
"I shall do what I can, my Master," said the earthen lamp.

"谁来接替我的职责？"落日问道。
"我愿竭尽所能，我的主人。"瓦灯回答。

154

By plucking her petals you do not gather the beauty of the flower.

花瓣可采撷，美丽不可得。

155

Silence will carry your voice like the nest that holds the sleeping birds.

沉默会传达你的声音,如鸟巢保护着睡鸟。

156

The Great walks with the Small without fear.
The Middling keeps aloof.

伟大不惧与渺小同行,半吊子高高在上。

157

The night opens the flowers in secret and allows the day to get thanks.

黑夜将花儿悄悄绽放,却让白昼领受赞赏。

158

Power takes as ingratitude the writhings of its victims.

强权把受害者的痛苦挣扎当作忘恩负义。

159

When we rejoice in our fulness, then we can part with our fruits with joy.

当我们以人生的丰盈为乐,便能欣然舍弃我们的果实。

160

The raindrops kissed the earth and whispered, —"We are thy homesick children, mother, come back to thee from the heaven."

雨滴亲吻着大地,轻声说:"妈妈,我们是思乡的孩子,从天堂回到你的怀抱。"

161

The cobweb pretends to catch dewdrops and catches flies.

蛛网假装要捕捉露珠,却捕住了苍蝇。

162

Love! When you come with the burning lamp of pain in your hand, I can see your face and know you as bliss.

爱啊!当你手提点燃的痛苦之灯走来,我能看见你的脸,并以你为幸福。

163

"The learned say that your lights will one day be no more." said the firefly to the stars.

The stars made no answer.

萤火虫对群星说:"学者说你的光芒终有一天会黯淡。"
群星默然不答。

164

In the dusk of the evening the bird of some early dawn comes to the nest of my silence.

在黄昏的薄暮中,有那清晨的鸟儿来到我宁静的巢中。

165

Thoughts pass in my mind like flocks of ducks in the sky.
I hear the voice of their wings.

思绪掠过我心头,如一群野鸭掠过天空。
我听到了它们振翅的声音。

166

The canal loves to think that rivers exist solely to supply it with water.

水渠一厢情愿地认为,河流的存在就是为它供水。

167

The world has kissed my soul with its pain, asking for its return in songs.

世界以痛苦吻我的灵魂，却要我报之以歌声。

168

That which oppresses me, is it my soul trying to come out in the open, or the soul of the world knocking at my heart for its entrance?

那压抑着我的，是我试图突围出去的灵魂，还是世界的灵魂正叩击我的心门想要进来？

169

Thought feeds itself with its own words and grows.

思想用自己的语言哺育自己并成长。

170

I have dipped the vessel of my heart into this silent hour; it has filled with love.

把我心的杯盏浸入宁静的时光,便盛满了爱。

171

Either you have work or you have not.

When you have to say, "Let us do something," then begins mischief.

不论是否有事情要做。

当你不得已说"让我们做点什么",就开始胡闹了。

172

The sunflower blushed to own the nameless flower as her kin.

The sun rose and smiled on it, saying, "Are you well, my darling?"

向日葵羞于认无名小花为亲属。

太阳升起,对它微笑着说:"你好吗,亲爱的?"

173

"Who drives me forward like fate?"
"The Myself striding on my back."

"是谁如命运驱使我前行？"
"是我自己在身后大步前进。"

174

The clouds fill the watercups of the river, hiding themselves in the distant hills.

云朵斟满河流的杯盏，自己悄然隐身于远山。

175

I spill water from my water jar as I walk on my way,
Very little remains for my home.

我一路走来，水从罐子里洒出，只剩下一点点带回家。

176

The water in a vessel is sparkling; the water in the sea is dark.
The small truth has words that are clear; the great truth has great silence.

杯水透亮，海水幽暗。
小道行文，大道不言。

177

Your smile was the flowers of your own fields, your talk was the rustle of your own mountain pines, but your heart was the woman that we all know.

你的微笑是你园中的花朵,你的言语是你林中的松涛,但你的心是我们全都熟悉的那个女人。

178

It is the little things that I leave behind for my loved ones, great things are for everyone.

小玩意留给爱人,大礼物赠予众生。

179

Woman, thou hast encircled the world's heart with the depth of thy tears as the sea has the earth.

女人,你用深沉的泪水包围世界的心,如汪洋环绕大地。

180

The sunshine greets me with a smile. The rain, his sad sister, talks to my heart.

阳光对我笑脸相迎。雨滴,他忧伤的妹妹,与我谈心。

181

My flower of the day dropped its petals forgotten.
In the evening it ripens into a golden fruit of memory.

白天，我的花抛弃被遗忘的花瓣。
夜晚，它成熟为金色的记忆之果。

182

I am like the road in the night listening to the footfalls of its memories in silence.

我像夜间的小路，在寂静中聆听记忆的足音。

183

The evening sky to me is like a window, and a lighted lamp, and a waiting behind it.

对我而言，夜空仿佛是一扇窗户，一盏明灯，灯后的一份期待。

184

He who is too busy doing good finds no time to be good.

忙于行善，无暇修身。

185

I am the autumn cloud, empty of rain, see my fullness in the field of ripened rice.

我是秋天的云彩,倾尽了所有雨露,从黄熟的稻田里,可以看见我生命的充盈。

186

They hated and killed and men praised them.
But God in shame hastens to hide its memory under the green grass.

他们挑起仇恨、制造杀戮,人们顶礼膜拜。
但是上帝感到羞愧,匆匆把记忆掩埋在绿草下。

187

Toes are the fingers that have forsaken their past.

脚趾是舍弃了过往的手指。

188

Darkness travels towards light, but blindness towards death.

黑暗驶往光明，盲目通向死亡。

189

The pet dog suspects the universe for scheming to take its place.

宠物狗忧心宇宙取其代之。

190

Sit still my heart, do not raise your dust.
Let the world find its way to you.

心啊，静下来，不要扬起尘土。
让世界找到通往你的路。

191

The bow whispers to the arrow before it speeds forth—"Your freedom is mine."

弓对离弦之箭说:"你的自由是我的。"

192

Woman, in your laughter you have the music of the fountain of life.

女人,你的笑声里有生命之泉的欢歌。

193

A mind all logic is like a knife all blade.
It makes the hand bleed that uses it.

过于理智的心如无柄之刀。
它会让使用者的手流血。

194

God loves man's lamp lights better than his own great stars.

神爱人间璀璨的灯火甚于自己伟大的群星。

195

This world is the world of wild storms kept tame with the music of beauty.

这世界是一个狂风暴雨被音乐之美驯服了的世界。

196

"My heart is like the golden casket of thy kiss," said the sunset cloud to the sun.

晚霞对落日说:"被你亲吻后,我的心像一个黄金宝盒。"

197

By touching you may kill, by keeping away you may possess.

近触易致伤害,远离或能拥有。

198

The cricket's chirp and the patter of rain come to me through the dark, like the rustle of dreams from my past youth.

蟋蟀嘶鸣,雨声淅沥,穿过黑暗来到我身边,仿佛逝去的青春年华的梦呓。

199

"I have lost my dewdrop," cries the flower to the morning sky that has lost all its stars.

"我丢失了我的露珠。"花儿清晨对刚失尽群星的天空哭诉。

200

The burning log bursts in flame and cries, —"This is my flower, my death."

燃烧的木块绽出烈焰,叫道:"这是我的花朵,我的死亡。"

201

The wasp thinks that the honey-hive of the neighbouring bees is too small.

His neighbours ask him to build one still smaller.

黄蜂认为邻居蜜蜂的巢太小。

他的邻居让他建一个更小的。

202

"I cannot keep your waves," says the bank to the river.

"Let me keep your footprints in my heart."

河岸对河流说:"我留不住你的波浪。"

"那就让我把你的足迹留在心里。"

203

The day, with the noise of this little earth, drowns the silence of all worlds.

白昼以小小寰球的喧嚣，淹没了整个宇宙的静默。

204

The song feels the infinite in the air, the picture in the earth, the poem in the air and the earth;

For its words have meaning that walks and music that soars.

歌声在天空感受无限，画卷在大地感受无限，诗歌在天空与大地感受无限；

因为诗句既有意念的奔跑，又有音乐的飞翔。

205

When the sun goes down to the West, the East of his morning stands before him in silence.

夕阳西下时分,他黎明的东方已悄然屹立在前面。

206

Let me not put myself wrongly to my world and set it against me.

别让我在自己的世界里错位,使其与我对立。

207

Praise shames me, for I secretly beg for it.

荣誉使我蒙羞,因为我曾暗中祈求。

208

Let my doing nothing when I have nothing to do become untroubled in its depth of peace like the evening in the seashore when the water is silent.

当我无事可做时,就让我什么都别做,沉浸在平静深处,不为所动,如波涛沉静时海边的黄昏。

209

Maiden, your simplicity, like the blueness of the lake, reveals your depth of truth.

少女,你的纯粹如湖水的湛蓝,呈现出真理的深邃。

210

The best does not come alone. It comes with the company of the all.

至善不会独来,而是伴随万物而至。

211

God's right hand is gentle, but terrible is his left hand.

神右手慈悲，左手霹雳。

212

My evening came among the alien trees and spoke in a language which my morning stars did not know.

我的黄昏从异域的林中走来，说着我的晨星听不懂的语言。

213

Night's darkness is a bag that bursts with the gold of the dawn.

夜晚的黑暗是一个口袋，透射出黎明的金光。

214

Our desire lends the colours of the rainbow to the mere mists and vapours of life.

我们的欲望，把彩虹的色彩借给缥缈的人生。

215

God waits to win back his own flowers as gifts from man's hands.

神等待着把他自己的花朵作为礼物，从人手上赢回去。

216

My sad thoughts tease me asking me their own names.

忧伤的思绪纠缠着我，追问他们自己的名字。

217

The service of the fruit is precious, the service of the flower is sweet, but let my service be the service of the leaves in its shade of humble devotion.

果实的奉献珍贵,鲜花的奉献芬芳,愿我的奉献是绿叶的奉献,投下谦卑的阴凉。

218

My heart has spread its sails to the idle winds for the shadowy island of Anywhere.

我的心向慵懒的风扬帆,想去往不知何处的荒岛。

219

Men are cruel, but Man is kind.

众人残酷,个人善良。

220

Make me thy cup and let my fulness be for thee and for thine.

把我当作你的杯盏,让我为你和你的人斟满。

221

The storm is like the cry of some god in pain whose love the earth refuses.

风暴如同天神的痛哭,因他的爱被大地拒绝。

222

The world does not leak because death is not a crack.

世界不会流逝,因为死亡不是裂谷。

223

Life has become richer by the love that has been lost.

生命因为失去的爱而变得更加富足。

224

My friend, your great heart shone with the sunrise of the East like the snowy summit of a lonely hill in the dawn.

我的朋友，你伟大的心灵，闪耀着日出东方的光辉，如积雪的孤峰傲立于黎明。

225

The fountain of death makes the still water of life play.

死亡的涌泉让生命的静水欢腾。

226

Those who have everything but thee, my God, laugh at those who have nothing but thyself.

我的天帝,那些除你之外拥有一切的人,在嘲笑除你之外一无所有的人。

227

The movement of life has its rest in its own music.

生命的运动在自己的韵律里休息。

228

Kicks only raise dust and not crops from the earth.

除了扬起尘土,踢足一无所获。

229

Our names are the light that glows on the sea waves at night and then dies without leaving its signature.

我们的名字如同夜间海浪的波光，消逝得了无踪迹。

230

Let him only see the thorns who has eyes to see the rose.

让那看到玫瑰的人也看到刺。

231

Set bird's wings with gold and it will never again soar in the sky.

给鸟儿的翅膀系上黄金,它便再也不能在天空翱翔。

232

The same lotus of our clime blooms here in the alien water with the same sweetness, under another name.

故乡的莲花在异域的水中绽放,一样的芬芳,不同的名字。

233

In heart's perspective the distance looms large.

从心中远望,相隔的距离更显辽阔。

234

The moon has her light all over the sky, her dark spots to herself.

月亮把清辉洒满天空,把黑斑留给自己。

235

Do not say, "It is morning," and dismiss it with a name of yesterday. See it for the first time as a new-born child that has no name.

不要说"这是清晨",不要用昨天的名字将其打发。把它看作一个初次看见的无名新生儿。

236

Smoke boasts to the sky, and Ashes to the earth, that they are brothers to the fire.

青烟向天空夸耀,灰烬向大地吹嘘,都自称是火的兄弟。

237

The raindrop whispered to the jasmine, "Keep me in your heart for ever."

The jasmine sighed, "Alas," and dropped to the ground.

雨滴对茉莉花轻声说:"把我永远存在你心里。"

"唉。"茉莉花叹息一声,落在地上。

238

Timid thoughts, do not be afraid of me.

I am a poet.

羞怯的灵感,别怕我。

我是一个诗人。

239

The dim silence of my mind seems filled with crickets' chirp—the grey twilight of sound.

在我黯然孤寂的心里,仿佛充满蟋蟀的鸣唱——灰暗垂暮的声音。

240

Rockets, your insult to the stars follows yourself back to the earth.

烟火,你对星空的侮辱,将与你一同坠回大地。

241

Thou hast led me through my crowded travels of the day to my evening's loneliness.

I wait for its meaning through the stillness of the night.

你领着我穿越白天熙攘的旅程,抵达黄昏的孤寂。
在夜晚的沉静中,我期待着它的意义。

242

This life is the crossing of a sea, where we meet in the same narrow ship.

In death we reach the shore and go to our different worlds.

今生如同渡海,我们相逢在一叶扁舟。
死时我们抵达彼岸,去往各自的世界。

243

The stream of truth flows through its channels of mistakes.

真理之水流过谬误之渠。

244

My heart is homesick today for the one sweet hour across the sea of time.

今天，我的心思乡了，为了那穿越时间之海的甜蜜时刻。

245

The bird-song is the echo of the morning light back from the earth.

鸟儿的欢歌,是晨光从大地反射的回音。

246

"Are you too proud to kiss me?" the morning light asks the buttercup.

晨曦问金凤花:"你骄傲得不肯吻我么?"

247

"How may I sing to thee and worship, O Sun?" asked the little flower.

"By the simple silence of thy purity," answered the sun.

"太阳,我要怎样歌颂你?"小花问道。
"用你纯洁的沉默。"太阳回答。

248

Man is worse than an animal when he is an animal.

人若为兽,禽兽不如。

249

Dark clouds become heaven's flowers when kissed by light.

乌云被光明一吻,便化作天堂的花朵。

250

Let not the sword-blade mock its handle for being blunt.

莫让剑锋嘲笑剑柄之钝。

251

The night's silence, like a deep lamp, is burning with the light of its milky way.

夜晚的静默如一盏深深的灯,燃着银河之光。

252

Around the sunny island of Life swells day and night death's limitless song of the sea.

生命的阳光之岛周围,日夜汹涌着大海无尽的死亡之歌。

253

Is not this mountain like a flower, with its petals of hill, drinking the sunlight?

山峰如花瓣饮着阳光,不正像一朵花吗?

254

The real with its meaning read wrong and emphasis misplaced is the unreal.

真的本意被曲解,本末被倒置,就成了假。

255

Find your beauty, my heart, from the world's movement, like the boat that has the grace of the wind and the water.

我的心，从世界的律动中寻找你的美，如小船拥有清风和流水的优雅。

256

The eyes are not proud of their sight but of their eyeglasses.

眼睛不以视力为傲，却以眼镜为傲。

257

I live in this little world of mine and am afraid to make it the least less. Lift me into thy world and let me have the freedom gladly to lose my all.

我蜗居在我狭小的世界,生怕它变得更小。把我升入你的世界,让我拥有欣然失去一切的自由。

258

The false can never grow into truth by growing in power.

谬误永远不能凭借附生于强权而成为真理。

259

My heart, with its lapping waves of song, longs to caress this green world of the sunny day.

我的心,随着它拍岸的歌声之潮,渴望轻抚这晴朗的绿色世界。

260

Wayside grass, love the star, then your dreams will come out in flowers.

路边的小草,爱上星星吧,你的梦想便会在花朵里实现。

261

Let your music, like a sword, pierce the noise of the market to its heart.

让你的音乐如一柄利剑,直刺闹市的心脏。

262

The trembling leaves of this tree touch my heart like the fingers of an infant child.

这棵树摇曳的叶子,如婴儿的手指触摸着我的心。

263

The sadness of my soul is her bride's veil.
It waits to be lifted in the night.

我灵魂深处的忧伤,像新娘的面纱,等着在夜里被撩起。

264

The little flower lies in the dust.
It sought the path of the butterfly.

小花睡在尘埃里,寻觅蝴蝶的踪迹。

265

I am in the world of the roads. The night comes. Open thy gate, thou world of the home.

我在这阡陌交错的世上。夜幕降临,开门吧,家的世界。

266

I have sung the songs of thy day. In the evening let me carry thy lamp through the stormy path.

我已唱过你白昼的歌。在夜晚,让我举着你的灯走过风雨之路。

267

I do not ask thee into the house.
Come into my infinite loneliness, my Lover.

我不要求你走进我的屋里。
请进入我无尽的孤独中,我的爱人。

268

Death belongs to life as birth does. The walk is in the raising of the foot as in the laying of it down.

死亡属于生命,如同新生;行走既在举足,也在落足。

269

I have learnt the simple meaning of thy whispers in flowers and sunshine—teach me to know thy words in pain and death.

我已领悟你在花朵与阳光里低语的意义——请教我领会你在痛苦和死亡中的话语。

270

The night's flower was late when the morning kissed her, she shivered and sighed and dropped to the ground.

夜晚的花朵姗姗来迟,当清晨吻她,她战栗着,叹息一声,凋落在地上。

271

Through the sadness of all things I hear the crooning of the Eternal Mother.

透过万物的悲伤,我听见永恒之母的沉吟。

272

I came to your shore as a stranger, I lived in your house as a guest, I leave your door as a friend, my earth.

大地,作为生人我登临你岸,作为宾客我住进你家,作为朋友我离开你门。

273

Let my thoughts come to you, when I am gone, like the afterglow of sunset at the margin of starry silence.

当我离去,让我的思想走近你,如落日余晖在那寂静星空的边际。

274

Light in my heart the evening star of rest and then let the night whisper to me of love.

点燃我心中安闲的星灯,让夜晚对我轻声爱语。

275

I am a child in the dark.

I stretch my hands through the coverlet of night for thee, Mother.

我是一个黑暗中的孩子。

我从夜的帷幕里向您伸出双手,母亲。

276

The day of work is done. Hide my face in your arms, Mother. Let me dream.

白天的工作已完成。把我的脸藏在您的臂弯里,母亲。

让我安然入梦。

277

The lamp of meeting burns long; it goes out in a moment at the parting.

聚会之灯长明,散时骤然熄灭。

278

One word keep for me in thy silence, O World, when I am dead, "I have loved."

世界啊,当我死去,请在你的沉默中为我留下一句:"我爱过"。

279

We live in this world when we love it.

我们热爱世界，才活在其中。

280

Let the dead have the immortality of fame, but the living the immortality of love.

让死者享有不朽之名，而生者享有永恒之爱。

281

I have seen thee as the half-awakened child sees his mother in the dusk of the dawn and then smiles and sleeps again.

我看见你,像半醒的婴儿在微弱的晨光里看见他的母亲,又微笑着安然入睡。

282

I shall die again and again to know that life is inexhaustible.

我愿九死不悔,探求生无止境。

283

While I was passing with the crowd in the road I saw thy smile from the balcony and I sang and forgot all noise.

当我随着路上拥挤的人潮,望见你在阳台上嫣然一笑,我唱起歌,忘了所有喧嚣。

284

Love is life in its fulness like the cup with its wine.

爱是丰盈的生命,如杯盏盛满美酒。

285

They light their own lamps and sing their own words in their temples.

But the birds sing thy name in thine own morning light,—for thy name is joy.

他们在寺庙里,点燃自己的灯,吟唱自己的经文。

但鸟儿在你清晨中歌唱你的名字——因为你的名字便是欢乐。

286

Lead me in the centre of thy silence to fill my heart with songs.

领我到你静寂的中心,使我心中充满歌声。

287

Let them live who choose in their own hissing world of fireworks.

My heart longs for thy stars, my God.

让那些选择在他们烟花嘶鸣的自我世界里的,就生活在那里吧。

我的心向往着你的星辰,我的天帝。

288

Love's pain sang round my life like the unplumbed sea, and love's joy sang like birds in its flowering groves.

爱的痛苦如莫测的海洋环绕我的一生歌唱,而爱的欢乐如鸟儿在花丛中歌唱。

289

Put out the lamp when thou wishest.
I shall know thy darkness and shall love it.

如果你愿意,就把灯熄灭。
我会懂你的黑暗,并爱上它。

290

When I stand before thee at the day's end thou shalt see my scars and know that I had my wounds and also my healing.

当岁月将尽,我站在你面前,你会看见我的伤痕,了解我的创伤以及我的愈合。

291

Some day I shall sing to thee in the sunrise of some other world, "I have seen thee before in the light of the earth, in the love of man."

有一天，我将在另一个世界的晨曦里对你歌唱："我见过你，在地球的光中，在世人的爱里。"

292

Clouds come floating into my life from other days no longer to shed rain or usher storm but to give colour to my sunset sky.

往日的云彩飘进我的生活，不再有雨，不再有风，只为我夕阳下的天空添彩。

293

Truth raises against itself the storm that scatters its seeds broadcast.

真理引发反对自己的风暴,把它的种子撒遍天涯海角。

294

The storm of the last night has crowned this morning with golden peace.

昨夜的风雨用金色的和平为今天的清晨加冕。

295

Truth seems to come with its final word; and the final word gives birth to its next.

真理仿佛带来了定论；而定论又衍生了下一个。

296

Blessed is he whose fame does not outshine his truth.

名副其实的人是有福的。

297

Sweetness of thy name fills my heart when I forget mine—like thy morning sun when the mist is melted.

你甜美的名字充满我内心，使我忘了自己的名字——如同当你的朝阳升起，晨雾便散去。

298

The silent night has the beauty of the mother and the clamorous day of the child.

静夜如母亲的娴静，白昼如孩子的嬉闹。

299

The world loved man when he smiled. The world became afraid of him when he laughed.

当人微笑，世界爱他；当人大笑，世界害怕。

300

God waits for man to regain his childhood in wisdom.

神期望人在智慧中重获童年。

301

Let me feel this world as thy love taking form, then my love will help it.

让我感知到这个世界是你的爱正在成形,那么我的爱也将帮助它。

302

Thy sunshine smiles upon the winter days of my heart, never doubting of its spring flowers.

你的阳光向我心中的冬天微笑,从不怀疑春天的花朵即将来到。

303

God kisses the finite in his love and man the infinite.

神在他的爱中亲吻有限,而人亲吻无限。

304

Thou crossest desert lands of barren years to reach the moment of fulfilment.

你穿越时光的荒漠,抵达圆满的瞬间。

305

God's silence ripens man's thoughts into speech.

神的静默使人的思想圆熟为语言。

306

Thou wilt find, Eternal Traveller, marks of thy footsteps across my songs.

永恒的过客,你将在我的颂歌里找到你的足迹。

307

Let me not shame thee, Father, who displayest thy glory in thy children.

让我不使您蒙羞,父亲,您的光荣将显现在您的孩子们身上。

308

Cheerless is the day, the light under frowning clouds is like a punished child with traces of tears on its pale cheeks, and the cry of the wind is like the cry of a wounded world. But I know I am travelling to meet my Friend.

天气阴沉,光在蹙眉的云下,像一个被责罚的孩子,苍白的脸上挂着泪痕,风呼啸着,像一个受伤世界的哀鸣。但我知道,我正跋涉在会见朋友的路上。

309

To-night there is a stir among the palm leaves, a swell in the sea, Full Moon, like the heart throb of the world. From what unknown sky hast thou carried in thy silence the aching secret of love?

今晚,棕榈叶萧萧,海浪汹涌,满月高悬,如世界的心悸。从什么未知的天空里,你从沉默里带来爱的痛苦的秘密?

310

I dream of a star, an island of light, where I shall be born and in the depth of its quickening leisure my life will ripen its works like the ricefield in the autumn sun.

我梦见一颗星,一个光明之岛,我将在那里出生,我的生命将在它飞逝的闲暇深处,圆熟一生的事业,如秋日阳光下的稻田。

311

The smell of the wet earth in the rain rises like a great chant of praise from the voiceless multitude of the insignificant.

大地湿润的气息从雨中升腾，如伟大的赞歌发自沉默的众生。

312

That love can ever lose is a fact that we cannot accept as truth.

爱情也会失去，是一个我们不愿接受的事实。

313

We shall know some day that death can never rob us of that which our soul has gained, for her gains are one with herself.

有一天，我们终将明白，死亡也夺不走我们灵魂的收获，因为他们已融为一体。

314

God comes to me in the dusk of my evening with the flowers from my past kept fresh in his basket.

神在黄昏的幽暗里来到我面前，带着我往日的花朵，在他的篮子里鲜艳如初。

315

When all the strings of my life will be tuned, my Master, then at every touch of thine will come out the music of love.

主啊,当我的生命之弦都已调和,你的每一次触碰,都会弹出爱的乐章。

316

Let me live truly, my Lord, so that death to me become true.

让我真诚地生活,我的主人,这样我就能直面死亡。

317

Man's history is waiting in patience for the triumph of the insulted man.

人类的历史在坚忍地等待受辱者的胜利。

318

I feel thy gaze upon my heart this moment like the sunny silence of the morning upon the lonely field whose harvest is over.

此刻，我感到你的目光投在我心田，如清晨阳光明媚的寂静落在收割后孤寂的田野上。

319

I long for the Island of Songs across this heaving Sea of Shouts.

我渴望有音乐之岛，穿越汹涌的咆哮之海。

320

The prelude of the night is commenced in the music of the sunset, in its solemn hymn to the ineffable dark.

夜的序曲始于夕阳的乐章，向不可形容的黑暗致以庄严的颂歌。

321

I have scaled the peak and found no shelter in fame's bleak and barren height. Lead me, my Guide, before the light fades, into the valley of quiet where life's harvest mellows into golden wisdom.

我登上顶峰,发现在盛名荒芜凄凉的高处,竟没有容身之地。我的向导,请在光明逝去前,领我进入宁静的山谷,在那里,我一生的收获将圆熟为金色的智慧。

322

Things look phantastic in this dimness of the dusk—the spires whose bases are lost in the dark and tree tops like blots of ink. I shall wait for the morning and wake up to see thy city in the light.

在黄昏的朦胧中,万物如梦,塔基消融在黑暗里,树梢如斑驳墨迹。我等待着黎明,醒来的时候,在光明里看见你的城市。

323

I have suffered and despaired and known death and I am glad that I am in this great world.

我受过苦难，有过绝望，尝过死亡，但庆幸我依然活在这伟大的世上。

324

There are tracts in my life that are bare and silent. They are the open spaces where my busy days had their light and air.

我生命中那贫瘠和寂寥的荒原，是我奔忙日子里汲取阳光和空气的旷野。

325

Release me from my unfulfilled past clinging to me from behind making death difficult.

不圆满的过往从身后缠住我，使我难以安然赴死，放开我吧。

326

Let this be my last word, that I trust in thy love.

就以这首诗结束："我相信你的爱。"

吉檀迦利
Gitanjali

1

Thou hast made me endless, such is thy pleasure. This frail vessel thou emptiest again and again, and fillest it ever with fresh life.

This little flute of a reed thou hast carried over hills and dales, and hast breathed through it melodies eternally new.

At the immortal touch of thy hands my little heart loses its limits in joy and gives birth to utterance ineffable.

Thy infinite gifts come to me only on these very small hands of mine. Ages pass, and still thou pourest, and still there is room to fill.

你使我延续不尽，这是你的乐趣。你反复倾空这薄脆的杯盏，又以新的生命注满。

你携着这小小的芦笛翻山越谷，吹出永新的乐章。

在你双手不朽的轻抚下，我卑微的心在欢乐中突破极限，发出不可言喻的声响。

你无尽的赐予，只注入我微小的手掌。时代流逝，你倾注不止，而我的手中仍有余量。

2

When thou commandest me to sing it seems that my heart would break with pride; and I look to thy face, and tears come to my eyes.

All that is harsh and dissonant in my life melts into one sweet harmony—and my adoration spreads wings like a glad bird on its flight across the sea.

I know thou takest pleasure in my singing. I know that only as a singer I come before thy presence.

I touch by the edge of the far spreading wing of my song thy feet which I could never aspire to reach.

Drunk with the joy of singing I forget myself and call thee friend who art my lord.

当你吩咐我歌唱，我的心骄傲欲裂，我望着你的脸庞，泪水涌出眼眶。

我生命中所有的嘈杂与不谐融成甜美的和声——我的敬慕如一只欢快的鸟儿展翅飞越汪洋。

我知道你欣赏我的歌唱。我知道只有身为歌者，才能来到你身旁。

我用歌声远远伸展的翅梢触碰你的双脚,那是我从不奢望触及的。

沉醉在歌唱的喜悦中,我忘了自己,与你朋友相称,而你本是我的主人。

3

I know not how thou singest, my master! I ever listen in silent amazement.

The light of thy music illumines the world. The life breath of thy music runs from sky to sky. The holy stream of thy music breaks through all stony obstacles and rushes on.

My heart longs to join in thy song, but vainly struggles for a voice. I would speak, but speech breaks not into song, and I cry out baffled. Ah, thou hast made my heart captive in the endless meshes of thy music, my master!

我的主人,我不知道你怎么歌唱!我总是在静静的惊奇中聆听。

你音乐的光辉普照世界,你音乐的生气传遍诸天,你音乐的圣泉冲破一切坚固的阻挡奔流而去。

我的心渴望融入你的歌声,却挣扎不出一丝声音。我想说话,但言不成调,甚至无法呼喊。啊,你已将我的心俘获在你无尽的音乐之网中,我的主人!

4

Life of my life, I shall ever try to keep my body pure, knowing that thy living touch is upon all my limbs.

I shall ever try to keep all untruths out from my thoughts, knowing that thou art that truth which has kindled the light of reason in my mind.

I shall ever try to drive all evils away from my heart and keep my love in flower, knowing that thou hast thy seat in the inmost shrine of my heart.

And it shall be my endeavour to reveal thee in my actions, knowing it is thy power gives me strength to act.

我生命的生命，我要永远保持身体的纯洁，因为我知道是你鲜活的轻抚遍布我的周身。

我要竭力摒弃我思想中的一切虚伪，因为我知道你就是点亮我心中理智之光的真理。

我要竭力驱除我心中的一切邪恶，让我的爱绽放如花，因为我知道你的座席已安放在我内心深处的圣殿。

我要竭力在行动中彰显你，因为我知道是你的神威赐我行动的力量。

5

I ask for a moment's indulgence to sit by thy side. The works that I have in hand I will finish afterwards.

Away from the sight of thy face my heart knows no rest nor respite, and my work becomes an endless toil in a shoreless sea of toil.

To-day the summer has come at my window with its sighs and murmurs; and the bees are playing their minstrelsy at the court of the flowering grove.

Now it is time to sit quiet, face to face with thee, and to sing dedication of live in this silent and overflowing leisure.

我请求坐在你身旁放松片刻。手头的劳作，我稍后再完成。

看不见你的面容，我的心无法休息和舒缓，我的劳作变成无边苦海中无尽的苦役。

今天，夏日来到我的窗前浅叹低吟；蜂群在林花绽放的庭院中吟唱。

此刻正好静静地坐下，与你面对面，在这宁静而悠长的闲暇中，唱起生命的赞歌。

6

Pluck this little flower and take it, delay not! I fear lest it droop and drop into the dust.

It may not find a place in thy garland, but honour it with a touch of pain from thy hand and pluck it. I fear lest the day end before I am aware, and the time of offering go by.

Though its colour be not deep and its smell be faint, use this flower in thy service and pluck it while there is time.

请摘下这朵小花带走,不要耽搁!我怕它凋落在尘埃里。

也许它配不上你的花环,但请你伸手将其采摘,以触碰的疼痛赐它荣耀。我担心在我醒来前,白昼已逝,错过供奉的时辰。

虽然它颜色不艳,香气清淡,请用这花朵供奉,及时将其采摘。

7

My song has put off her adornments. She has no pride of dress and decoration. Ornaments would mar our union; they would come between thee and me; their jingling would drown thy whispers.

My poet's vanity dies in shame before thy sight. O master poet, I have sat down at thy feet. Only let me make my life simple and straight, like a flute of reed for thee to fill with music.

我的歌卸下妆饰。她不再以衣饰为傲。妆饰妨碍我们融为一体,它们横亘在你我之间,叮叮当当的声响淹没了你的细语。

在你面前,我那诗人的虚荣在羞愧中消逝。诗圣啊,我坐在你脚下。就让我的生命简单直率,如一支芦笛,由你用音乐充满。

8

The child who is decked with prince's robes and who has jewelled chains round his neck loses all pleasure in his play; his dress hampers him at every step.

In fear that it may be frayed, or stained with dust he keeps himself from the world, and is afraid even to move.

Mother, it is no gain, thy bondage of finery, if it keep one shut off from the healthful dust of the earth, if it rob one of the right of entrance to the great fair of common human life.

那个身穿王子冠服,颈戴珠宝项链的孩子,在游戏中失去了所有欢乐;他的服饰羁绊着他的每一步。

担心衣服破损,沾染尘土,他让自己与世隔绝,甚至不敢挪步。

母亲,如果你华美的束缚,让人和大地的沃土隔绝,剥夺人进入日常生活盛会的权利,将毫无益处。

9

O Fool, try to carry thyself upon thy own shoulders! O beggar, to come beg at thy own door!

Leave all thy burdens on his hands who can bear all, and never look behind in regret.

Thy desire at once puts out the light from the lamp it touches with its breath. It is unholy—take not thy gifts through its unclean hands. Accept only what is offered by sacred love.

傻瓜呀,竟想把自己扛在肩上!乞丐呀,竟来到自己门口乞讨!

将你的重担交给那能承担一切的双手,永远不要因后悔而回首。

你欲望的气息,会将触及的灯火瞬间吹灭。它是不圣洁的——不要从它不洁的手中拿取礼物。只领受神圣之爱的赐予。

10

Here is thy footstool and there rest thy feet where live the poorest, and lowliest, and lost.

When I try to bow to thee, my obeisance cannot reach down to the depth where thy feet rest among the poorest, and lowliest, and lost.

Pride can never approach to where thou walkest in the clothes of the humble among the poorest, and lowliest, and lost.

My heart can never find its way to where thou keepest company with the companionless among the poorest, the lowliest, and the lost.

这是你的脚榻,你在至贫至贱流离失所的人群中歇足。

我想向你鞠躬,我的敬意不能低到你歇足之所的深处,那至贫至贱流离失所的人群中。

你衣衫褴褛,走在至贫至贱流离失所的人群中,骄傲永远不能抵达那里。

你在至贫至贱流离失所的人群中与孤苦伶仃的人做伴,我的心永远找不到通往那里的路。

11

Leave this chanting and singing and telling of beads! Whom dost thou worship in this lonely dark corner of a temple with doors all shut? Open thine eyes and see thy God is not before thee!

He is there where the tiller is tilling the hard ground and where the pathmaker is breaking stones. He is with them in sun and in shower, and his garment is covered with dust. Put of thy holy mantle and even like him come down on the dusty soil!

Deliverance? Where is this deliverance to be found? Our master himself has joyfully taken upon him the bonds of creation; he is bound with us all for ever.

Come out of thy meditations and leave aside thy flowers and incense! What harm is there if thy clothes become tattered and stained? Meet him and stand by him in toil and in sweat of thy brow.

抛下诵经、吟唱和数珠吧!你在这门窗紧闭、孤寂幽暗的寺庙一角祭拜谁呢?睁眼看吧,神不在你面前!

他在耕耘贫瘠土地的农夫那里,在劈石筑路的工人那里。他和他们一起,在烈日下,在风雨中,衣袍沾满尘土。脱下你的圣袍,就像他一样,走到泥土里去吧!

解脱？哪里能得解脱？我们的主已欣然戴上创造的枷锁，他永远与我们紧密相连。

走出冥想，抛开鲜花和熏香！你的衣服污损又何妨？去迎接他，和他一起辛勤劳作，满头大汗。

12

The time that my journey takes is long and the way of it long.

I came out on the chariot of the first gleam of light, and pursued my voyage through the wildernesses of worlds leaving my track on many a star and planet.

It is the most distant course that comes nearest to thyself, and that training is the most intricate which leads to the utter simplicity of a tune.

The traveller has to knock at every alien door to come to his own, and one has to wander through all the outer worlds to reach the innermost shrine at the end.

My eyes strayed far and wide before I shut them and said "Here art thou!"

The question and the cry "Oh, where?" melt into tears of a thousand streams and deluge the world with the flood of the assurance "I am!"

我的旅程漫长，路途遥远。

我迎着第一缕晨曦驱车出行，穿越荒凉的世界，在无数星球上留下辙痕。

离你最近之处,路程最远;最简单的曲调,需要最繁复的训练。

旅人要敲遍每一扇陌生的门,才能找到自己的家;一个人要周游外界,最后才能抵达内心最深处的圣殿。

我放眼辽阔的远方,最后闭上眼说:"原来你在这里!"

"啊,你在哪里?"这疑问和呼喊化作千行泪流,汇进"我在这里!"那坚定回答的洪流,席卷了整个世界。

13

The song that I came to sing remains unsung to this day.

I have spent my days in stringing and in unstringing my instrument.

The time has not come true, the words have not been rightly set; only there is the agony of wishing in my heart.

The blossom has not opened; only the wind is sighing by.

I have not seen his face, nor have I listened to his voice; only I have heard his gentle footsteps from the road before my house.

The livelong day has passed in spreading his seat on the floor; but the lamp has not been lit and I cannot ask him into my house.

I live in the hope of meeting with him; but this meeting is not yet.

我要唱的歌，至今还未唱出。

我花费时日，反复调理琴弦。

时辰未到，歌词还未填妥；我心中只有痛切的愿望。

花蕾还未绽放；只有风叹息而过。

我没见过他的容颜，也未听过他的声音；我只听到他轻柔的脚步从我屋前的路上走过。

我一整天都在地上为他铺设座位；但灯还未点亮，我不能邀他进屋。

我生活在与他相见的希望中，但至今未能相见。

14

My desires are many and my cry is pitiful, but ever didst thou save me by hard refusals; and this strong mercy has been wrought into my life through and through.

Day by day thou art making me worthy of the simple, great gifts that thou gavest to me unasked—this sky and the light, this body and the life and the mind—saving me from perils of overmuch desire.

There are times when I languidly linger and times when I awaken and hurry in search of my goal; but cruelly thou hidest thyself from before me.

Day by day thou art making me worthy of thy full acceptance by refusing me ever and anon, saving me from perils of weak, uncertain desire.

我的欲望繁多，我的哭泣可怜，但你永远用坚定的拒绝拯救我；这强大的悲悯已彻底融入我的生命。

日复一日，你将我从放纵欲望的险境中拯救，让我更配得上你主动赐予的简单而伟大的礼物——这天空和光明，这身躯、生命和心灵。

有时我懈怠彷徨，有时我幡然醒悟，匆匆追寻目标；但你却冷酷地避开我。

日复一日，你不断拒绝我，将我从软弱不定的欲望险境中拯救，让我更配得上你完全的接纳。

15

I am here to sing thee songs. In this hall of thine I have a corner seat.

In thy world I have no work to do; my useless life can only break out in tunes without a purpose.

When the hour strikes for thy silent worship at the dark temple of midnight, command me, my master, to stand before thee to sing.

When in the morning air the golden harp is tuned, honour me, commanding my presence.

我来到这里为你歌唱。我的座位在你殿堂的角落。

在你的世界里我无事可做；我无用的生命只能发出漫无目的的歌声。

在幽暗的殿堂中，当子夜静默祈祷的钟声敲响，命令我吧，我的主人，让我站在你面前歌唱。

当金色竖琴在晨光中调和，请赐我荣耀，命我出场。

16

I have had my invitation to this world's festival, and thus my life has been blessed. My eyes have seen and my ears have heard.

It was my part at this feast to play upon my instrument, and I have done all I could.

Now, I ask, has the time come at last when I may go in and see thy face and offer thee my silent salutation?

我已收到世界盛会的请柬,我的生命因此受到祝福。我的眼睛已经见识过,耳朵已经聆听过。

我的任务是在宴会中演奏,我已竭尽全力。

现在,我问,这一刻是否终于来临,我能进去瞻仰你的容颜并默默致敬吗?

17

I am only waiting for love to give myself up at last into his hands. That is why it is so late and why I have been guilty of such omissions.

They come with their laws and their codes to bind me fast; but I evade them ever, for I am only waiting for love to give myself up at last into his hands.

People blame me and call me heedless; I doubt not they are right in their blame.

The market day is over and work is all done for the busy. Those who came to call me in vain have gone back in anger. I am only waiting for love to give myself up at last into his hands.

我只是守候着爱，最终将自己献到他手里。这就是我迟到并感到愧疚的原因。

他们用清规戒律紧紧束缚我，但我始终避而不见；因为我只是守候着爱，最终将自己献到他手里。

人们责备我不理不睬，我不否认他们的责备有道理。

集市已散，繁忙的劳作都已结束。召唤我的人白忙一趟，含怒而去。我只是等待着爱，最终将自己献到他手里。

18

Clouds heap upon clouds and it darkens. Ah, love, why dost thou let me wait outside at the door all alone?

In the busy moments of the noontide work I am with the crowd, but on this dark lonely day it is only for thee that I hope.

If thou showest me not thy face, if thou leavest me wholly aside, I know not how I am to pass these long, rainy hours.

I keep gazing on the far away gloom of the sky, and my heart wanders wailing with the restless wind.

云层堆积，天色昏暗。唉，爱人，你为何让我独自在门外等待？

中午劳作繁忙时，我与大伙在一起，但在这黑暗孤独的日子，我只期盼你。

若你不肯与我见面，若你将我完全晾在一边，我不知如何度过这漫长的雨天。

我不断凝望天际的阴云，我的心与不息的风一起彷徨哀叹。

19

If thou speakest not I will fill my heart with thy silence and endure it. I will keep still and wait like the night with starry vigil and its head bent low with patience.

The morning will surely come, the darkness will vanish, and thy voice pour down in golden streams breaking through the sky.

Then thy words will take wing in songs from every one of my birds' nests, and thy melodies will break forth in flowers in all my forest groves.

你若不说话,我就以你的沉默填满我的心,并安然承受。我静静地等待,如夜晚守候繁星,耐心地低着头。

黎明必至,黑暗终消,你的声音如金色泉流,划破长空,倾注而下。

那时,你的话语将从我每一个鸟巢中展翅成歌,你的旋律将在我所有树丛中绽放花朵。

20

On the day when the lotus bloomed, alas, my mind was straying, and I knew it not. My basket was empty and the flower remained unheeded.

Only now and again a sadness fell upon me, and I started up from my dream and felt a sweet trace of a strange fragrance in the south wind.

That vague sweetness made my heart ache with longing and it seemed to me that is was the eager breath of the summer seeking for its completion.

I knew not then that it was so near, that it was mine, and that this perfect sweetness had blossomed in the depth of my own heart.

唉，莲花盛开那天，我心神不定，却浑然不觉。我的花篮空空，却对花儿视而不见。

不时有一阵忧愁袭来，我从梦中惊醒，感到南风里有一股奇香的芳踪。

这朦胧的芬芳让我因渴望而心痛，我感觉那仿佛是夏日热切的气息追寻着它的圆满。

那时，我不知道它离我这么近，而且就属于我，不知道这完美的芬芳已在我心深处绽放。

21

I must launch out my boat. The languid hours pass by on the shore—Alas for me!

The spring has done its flowering and taken leave. And now with the burden of faded futile flowers I wait and linger.

The waves have become clamorous, and upon the bank in the shady lane the yellow leaves flutter and fall.

What emptiness do you gaze upon! Do you not feel a thrill passing through the air with the notes of the far away song floating from the other shore?

我必须撑船出行了。悠闲的时光都消磨在岸边——可怜的我呀!

花事已了,春天便匆匆辞别。如今我怀着花朵徒然凋零的沉痛等待、徘徊。

潮水渐渐喧哗,沿岸的林荫路上黄叶飘落。

你凝视的是什么虚空!难道你没有感到一丝震颤随着从对岸飘来的歌声从空中传来吗?

22

In the deep shadows of the rainy July, with secret steps, thou walkest, silent as night, eluding all watchers.

To-day the morning has closed its eyes, heedless of the insistent calls of the loud east wind, and a thick veil has been drawn over the ever-wakeful blue sky.

The woodlands have hushed their songs, and doors are all shut at every house. Thou art the solitary wayfarer in this deserted street. Oh my only friend, my best beloved, the gates are open in my house—do not pass by like a dream.

在阴雨七月的浓阴中,你踏着隐秘的脚步走来,悄然如夜,避开了所有守望者。

今天,清晨已闭上双眼,不理会东风呼啸不断的召唤,一张厚幕遮蔽了永远清醒的蓝天。

树林停止了歌唱,家家关闭了门窗。在这冷清的街上,你是独行的旅人。我唯一的朋友啊,我的至爱,我的家门对你敞开——不要像梦一样飘过。

23

Art thou abroad on this stormy night on thy journey of love, my friend? The sky groans like one in despair.

I have no sleep to-night. Ever and again I open my door and look out on the darkness, my friend!

I can see nothing before me. I wonder where lies thy path!

By what dim shore of the ink-black river, by what far edge of the frowning forest, through what mazy depth of gloom art thou threading thy course to come to me, my friend?

在这暴风雨夜,你还在外面继续爱的旅行吗,我的朋友?天空像绝望者在哀号。

我一夜无眠。我一次又一次开门向黑暗中张望,我的朋友!

我什么都看不见,我不知道你从哪条路来!

我的朋友,你怎么摸索到我这里来,是沿着墨黑的河岸,是绕过遥远的愁林,还是穿过曲折的幽径?

24

If the day is done, if birds sing no more, if the wind has flagged tired, then draw the veil of darkness thick upon me, even as thou hast wrapt the earth with the coverlet of sleep and tenderly closed the petals of the drooping lotus at dusk.

From the traveller, whose sack of provisions is empty before the voyage is ended, whose garment is torn and dust-laden, whose strength is exhausted, remove shame and poverty, and renew his life like a flower under the cover of thy kindly night.

若白昼已逝，鸟儿不再歌唱，风儿已经吹倦，请拉过黑暗的厚纱盖住我，正如黄昏时分，你以睡梦的锦被裹住大地，轻柔地合拢睡莲的花瓣。

旅人的行程未尽，但粮袋已空，衣衫褴褛，一身尘土，筋疲力尽，你消除了他的羞愧与窘迫，让他的生命如花朵一样在你仁慈的夜里复苏。

25

In the night of weariness let me give myself up to sleep without struggle, resting my trust upon thee.

Let me not force my flagging spirit into a poor preparation for thy worship.

It is thou who drawest the veil of night upon the tired eyes of the day to renew its sight in a fresher gladness of awakening.

在这困倦的夜晚,让我不再硬撑,把自己交给睡眠,完全信任你。

让我不再强振萎靡的精神为你准备一个草率的礼拜。

是你拉上夜幕盖住白日的倦眼,让它的目光在苏醒的鲜活喜悦中恢复神采。

26

He came and sat by my side but I woke not. What a cursed sleep it was, O miserable me!

He came when the night was still; he had his harp in his hands, and my dreams became resonant with its melodies.

Alas, why are my nights all thus lost? Ah, why do I ever miss his sight whose breath touches my sleep?

他过来坐在我身边,我却没有醒来。多么可恶的睡眠,唉,我真可怜!

他在静夜来临,手抚竖琴,我的梦与它的旋律共鸣。

唉,为何我的夜晚都这么流逝?啊,为何他的气息触及我的酣眠,我却总看不见他?

27

Light, oh where is the light? Kindle it with the burning fire of desire!

There is the lamp but never a flicker of a flame, —is such thy fate, my heart? Ah, death were better by far for thee!

Misery knocks at thy door, and her message is that thy lord is wakeful, and he calls thee to the love-tryst through the darkness of night.

The sky is overcast with clouds and the rain is ceaseless. I know not what this is that stirs in me, —I know not its meaning.

A moment's flash of lightning drags down a deeper gloom on my sight, and my heart gropes for the path to where the music of the night calls me.

Light, oh where is the light! Kindle it with the burning fire of desire! It thunders and the wind rushes screaming through the void. The night is black as a black stone. Let not the hours pass by in the dark. Kindle the lamp of love with thy life.

光明，光明在哪里？用渴望的烈焰将其点燃！

那里有一盏灯，但没有一丝火焰——我的心呀，难道这就是你的命运？啊，与其如此，不如死亡！

悲伤叩响你的门，她捎来口信说你的主人依然醒着，他召唤你穿越暗夜去赶赴爱的约会。

乌云蔽空，大雨不息。我不知是什么搅动我心——我不明其意。

刹那的闪电，在我眼前投下一道更深的暗影，我的心探寻着通往夜曲召唤我之处的路径。

光明，光明在哪里！用渴望的烈焰将其点燃！雷声轰鸣，狂风呼啸着掠过长空。夜色漆黑，宛如磐石。不要让时光在黑暗中虚度。用你的生命将爱之灯点燃！

28

Obstinate are the trammels, but my heart aches when I try to break them.

Freedom is all I want, but to hope for it I feel ashamed.

I am certain that priceless wealth is in thee, and that thou art my best friend, but I have not the heart to sweep away the tinsel that fills my room.

The shroud that covers me is a shroud of dust and death; I hate it, yet hug it in love.

My debts are large, my failures great, my shame secret and heavy; yet when I come to ask for my good, I quake in fear lest my prayer be granted.

罗网坚固,但我试图冲决它们时心就剧痛。

我只要自由,但对自由的期盼让我感到羞愧。

我确信无价之宝在你那里,而你是我最好的朋友,但我不忍心清除我满屋浮华的装饰。

尘埃与死亡之衣裹着我;我恨它,却又依恋地将其裹紧。

我的债务繁多,我的失败惨痛,我的耻辱隐秘而沉重;但当我来向你祈福时,我战栗不安,生怕我的祈求得到允诺。

29

He whom I enclose with my name is weeping in this dungeon. I am ever busy building this wall all around; and as this wall goes up into the sky day by day I lose sight of my true being in its dark shadow.

I take pride in this great wall, and I plaster it with dust and sand lest a least hole should be left in this name; and for all the care I take I lose sight of my true being.

被我用名号囚禁起来的那个人,正在牢笼中哭泣。日复一日,我不停地砌墙,随着高墙直上云霄,真我在暗影下消失不见。

我以这高墙为傲,用沙土抹严,唯恐这名号上留下一丝空隙,我费尽心思,却再也看不见真我。

30

I came out alone on my way to my tryst. But who is this that follows me in the silent dark?

I move aside to avoid his presence but I escape him not.

He makes the dust rise from the earth with his swagger; he adds his loud voice to every word that I utter.

He is my own little self, my lord, he knows no shame; but I am ashamed to come to thy door in his company.

我独自上路赴约。是谁在幽暗中尾随我?

我走到一边试图避开他,但摆脱不了。

他昂首阔步,扬起满地尘土;他把喊叫掺进我的每一句话。

他就是我的小我,我的主人,他毫无廉耻;但我很惭愧,与他一同来到你门前。

31

"Prisoner, tell me, who was it that bound you?"

"It was my master," said the prisoner. "I thought I could outdo everybody in the world in wealth and power, and I amassed in my own treasure-house the money due to my king. When sleep overcame me I lay upon the bed that was for my lord, and on waking up I found I was a prisoner in my own treasure-house."

"Prisoner, tell me, who was it that wrought this unbreakable chain?"

"It was I," said the prisoner, "who forged this chain very carefully. I thought my invincible power would hold the world captive leaving me in a freedom undisturbed. Thus night and day I worked at the chain with huge fires and cruel hard strokes. When at last the work was done and the links were complete and unbreakable, I found that it held me in its grip."

"囚徒,告诉我,是谁将你捆绑?"

"是我的主人,"囚徒说,"我以为我的财富和权力胜过世上任何人,我将国王的钱财聚敛在我自己的宝库。睡意袭来,我睡在主人床上,醒来发现我在自己的宝库里沦为囚徒。"

"囚徒，告诉我，是谁锻造了这坚不可摧的锁链？"

"是我，"囚徒说，"是我精心锻造的。我以为我不可战胜的权力能掌控世界，拥有不受侵犯的自由。我日夜不停，以烈火和酷击锻造锁链。完工时，这锁链浑然一体坚不可摧，我发现它已将我牢牢锁住。"

32

By all means they try to hold me secure who love me in this world. But it is otherwise with thy love which is greater than theirs, and thou keepest me free.

Lest I forget them they never venture to leave me alone. But day passes by after day and thou art not seen.

If I call not thee in my prayers, if I keep not thee in my heart, thy love for me still waits for my love.

世间那些爱我的人，用尽一切办法约束我。你的爱比他们的更伟大，却不是这样，你让我自由。

他们从不贸然离开我，生怕我忘记他们。但日复一日，你从未现身。

即便我祈祷时不呼唤你，即便我不将你放在心里，你对我的爱依然期待着我的爱。

33

When it was day they came into my house and said, "We shall only take the smallest room here."

They said, "We shall help you in the worship of your God and humbly accept only our own share in his grace"; and then they took their seat in a corner and they sat quiet and meek.

But in the darkness of night I find they break into my sacred shrine, strong and turbulent, and snatch with unholy greed the offerings from God's altar.

白天,他们走进我的屋子里说:"我们只占用最小的一间屋。"

他们说:"我们要帮你祭拜你的天帝,只恭谦地领受我们那一份恩赐。"然后他们就安静恭顺地坐在屋角。

但黑夜里,我发现他们强行闯入我的圣殿,贪婪地攫取祭坛上的祭品。

34

Let only that little be left of me whereby I may name thee my all.

Let only that little be left of my will whereby I may feel thee on every side, and come to thee in everything, and offer to thee my love every moment.

Let only that little be left of me whereby I may never hide thee.

Let only that little of my fetters be left whereby I am bound with thy will, and thy purpose is carried out in my life—and that is the fetter of thy love.

只要我一息尚存,我就将你当作我的一切。

只要我一念尚存,我就能从四周感受你,凡事都请教你,时刻将我的爱献给你。

只要我一息尚存,我就永不隐藏你。

只要我的锁链还有一环尚存,我就和你的意志紧密相连,你的意愿在我身上实现——这锁链就是你的爱。

35

Where the mind is without fear and the head is held high;

Where knowledge is free;

Where the world has not been broken up into fragments by narrow domestic walls;

Where words come out from the depth of truth;

Where tireless striving stretches its arms towards perfection;

Where the clear stream of reason has not lost its way into the dreary desert sand of dead habit;

Where the mind is led forward by thee into ever-widening thought and action—

Into that heaven of freedom, my Father, let my country awake.

在那里，心无畏惧，头颅高昂；

在那里，知识即自由；

在那里，世界没有被家国的窄墙分割成碎片；

在那里，话语源自真理深处；

在那里，不懈的奋斗向完美伸出双臂；

在那里，理性的清泉没有迷失在积弊的荒漠；

在那里，心在你的指引下走向不断拓宽的思想和行动——

进入那自由的天国，天父啊，请让我的国家觉醒。

36

This is my prayer to thee, my lord—strike, strike at the root of penury in my heart.

Give me the strength lightly to bear my joys and sorrows.

Give me the strength to make my love fruitful in service.

Give me the strength never to disown the poor or bend my knees before insolent might.

Give me the strength to raise my mind high above daily trifles.

And give me the strength to surrender my strength to thy will with love.

我的主人,这是我对你的祈求——请你铲除,铲除我心中贫乏的根源。

赐我力量,让我从容承受欢乐和悲伤。

赐我力量,让我的爱在服务中丰收。

赐我力量,让我永不抛弃贫贱也不屈服于强权。

赐我力量,让我的心灵超脱日常琐事。

再赐我力量,让我的力量满怀爱意遵从你的意志。

37

I thought that my voyage had come to its end at the last limit of my power,—that the path before me was closed, that provisions were exhausted and the time come to take shelter in a silent obscurity.

But I find that thy will knows no end in me. And when old words die out on the tongue, new melodies break forth from the heart; and where the old tracks are lost, new country is revealed with its wonders.

我以为我的精力已竭,旅程将终——前路断绝,存粮耗尽,是时候寻一方幽境藏身了。

但我发现你的意志在我身上没有终点。陈言在舌尖上死去,新乐又从心中迸出。旧辙痕消逝之处,新田野又奇妙展现。

38

That I want thee, only thee—let my heart repeat without end. All desires that distract me, day and night, are false and empty to the core.

As the night keeps hidden in its gloom the petition for light, even thus in the depth of my unconsciousness rings the cry—I want thee, only thee.

As the storm still seeks its end in peace when it strikes against peace with all its might, even thus my rebellion strikes against thy love and still its cry is—I want thee, only thee.

我需要你，只需要你——让我心中不停地重复。那日夜诱惑我的所有欲望，都是彻底的荒谬和空虚。

就像黑夜隐藏在祈求光明的昏暗中，在我潜意识的深处仍回荡着呼喊——我需要你，只需要你。

正如风暴竭尽全力打破平静，却寻求止于平静，即便我的反叛抗击你的爱，它的呼喊仍是——我需要你，只需要你。

39

When the heart is hard and parched up, come upon me with a shower of mercy.

When grace is lost from life, come with a burst of song.

When tumultuous work raises its din on all sides shutting me out from beyond, come to me, my lord of silence, with thy peace and rest.

When my beggarly heart sits crouched, shut up in a corner, break open the door, my king, and come with the ceremony of a king.

When desire blinds the mind with delusion and dust, O thou holy one, thou wakeful, come with thy light and thy thunder.

当心田坚硬焦枯,请降以慈悲的甘霖。

当生命失去光彩,请带来激情的欢歌。

当繁琐的劳作在四周喧腾,使我与世隔绝,我沉默的主,请带来平静与安歇。

当我乞求的心蜷坐在角落,我的王,请带着王者的威仪破门而入。

当欲望以虚妄和尘埃蒙蔽心灵,圣者啊,你依然清醒,请带着闪电和雷鸣降临。

40

The rain has held back for days and days, my God, in my arid heart. The horizon is fiercely naked—not the thinnest cover of a soft cloud, not the vaguest hint of a distant cool shower.

Send thy angry storm, dark with death, if it is thy wish, and with lashes of lightning startle the sky from end to end.

But call back, my lord, call back this pervading silent heat, still and keen and cruel, burning the heart with dire despair.

Let the cloud of grace bend low from above like the tearful look of the mother on the day of the father's wrath.

天帝，我干枯的心田，已经很多天没有雨水的滋润。天际惨然裸露——没有一片轻云遮盖，也没有一丝远雨欲来的凉意。

如果你愿意，请降下狂怒的暴风雨，带着死亡的黑暗，以猛烈的闪电震彻诸天。

我的主，但请你召回，召回这默默弥散的酷热，它沉重、凌厉、残酷，以恐怖的绝望灼烧人心。

让慈云从天而降，像父亲震怒时，母亲那含泪的目光。

41

Where dost thou stand behind them all, my lover, hiding thyself in the shadows? They push thee and pass thee by on the dusty road, taking thee for naught. I wait here weary hours spreading my offerings for thee, while passers-by come and take my flowers, one by one, and my basket is nearly empty.

The morning time is past, and the noon. In the shade of evening my eyes are drowsy with sleep. Men going home glance at me and smile and fill me with shame. I sit like a beggar maid, drawing my skirt over my face, and when they ask me, what it is I want, I drop my eyes and answer them not.

Oh, how, indeed, could I tell them that for thee I wait, and that thou hast promised to come. How could I utter for shame that I keep for my dowry this poverty. Ah, I hug this pride in the secret of my heart.

I sit on the grass and gaze upon the sky and dream of the sudden splendour of thy coming—all the lights ablaze, golden pennons flying over thy car, and they at the roadside standing agape, when they see thee come down from thy seat to raise me from the dust, and set at thy side this ragged beggar girl a-tremble with shame and pride, like a creeper in a summer breeze.

But time glides on and still no sound of the wheels of thy chariot. Many a procession passes by with noise and shouts and glamour of glory. Is it only thou who wouldst stand in the shadow silent and behind them all? And only I who would wait and weep and wear out my heart in vain longing?

我的爱人,你站在大伙身后的什么地方,把自己藏在阴影里?尘土飞扬的路上,他们推开你走过,无视你的存在。我在这里守候了很久,摆放好给你的礼物,行人路过,拿走我的鲜花,一朵又一朵,我的花篮几乎空了。

清晨已过,正午也过去了。暮色中,我睡眼蒙眬。回家的人们看着我笑,让我满心羞愧。我像一个乞丐一样坐下,拉过衣襟遮住脸,他们问我想要什么,我垂目不答。

啊,真的,难道我能告诉他们我在等你,而且你承诺会来。我怎么好意思说贫困就是我的嫁妆。唉,我只在心中的隐秘之处拥抱着这份骄傲。

我坐在草地上凝望天空,梦想着你突然来临时的辉煌——众彩交辉,车上金旗飞扬,行人站在路边,目瞪口呆,他们看着你走下宝座,将我从尘埃中扶起,让我坐在你身边,我这衣衫褴褛的女乞丐,既羞怯又自豪,浑身颤抖,像夏日微风中的藤蔓。

— 吉檀迦利 —

时光悄然流逝,依然没听到你的车轮声。许多仪仗队走过,喧闹欢呼,光彩夺目。难道你只愿默默站在众人背后的影子里?难道,我只能垂泪等待,将我的心消磨在徒劳的期盼中吗?

42

Early in the day it was whispered that we should sail in a boat, only thou and I, and never a soul in the world would know of this our pilgrimage to no country and to no end.

In that shoreless ocean, at thy silently listening smile my songs would swell in melodies, free as waves, free from all bondage of words.

Is the time not come yet? Are there works still to do? Lo, the evening has come down upon the shore and in the fading light the seabirds come flying to their nests.

Who knows when the chains will be off, and the boat, like the last glimmer of sunset, vanish into the night?

清晨，我们密约乘舟远航，只有你和我，世上没有人知道我们这没有方向和终点的旅程。

在那无边的海上，在你静静聆听的微笑中，我的歌声悠扬，自由如波浪，挣脱了字句的束缚。

时间还没到吗？还有事情要做吗？看呐，夜幕已笼罩海岸，海鸟在薄暮中飞向归巢。

谁知道这锁链何时打开，任这小船如落日余晖，消融在夜色中？

43

The day was when I did not keep myself in readiness for thee; and entering my heart unbidden even as one of the common crowd, unknown to me, my king, thou didst press the signet of eternity upon many a fleeting moment of my life.

And to-day when by chance I light upon them and see thy signature, I find they have lain scattered in the dust mixed with the memory of joys and sorrows of my trivial days forgotten.

Thou didst not turn in contempt from my childish play among dust, and the steps that I heard in my playroom are the same that are echoing from star to star.

我的国王,那天我没有做好迎接你的准备,你像一个素不相识的凡人,不请自来进入我心里,在我生命中无数飞逝的瞬间,铭上永恒的印记。

今天,我偶然照亮它们,看见你的印记,发现它们散落在尘埃里,混杂着我那些已淡忘的日常悲欢记忆。

你没有不屑地绕开我在尘土间的幼稚游戏,我在游戏房里听见的足音,与群星之间回荡的一样。

44

This is my delight, thus to wait and watch at the wayside where shadow chases light and the rain comes in the wake of the summer.

Messengers, with tidings from unknown skies, greet me and speed along the road. My heart is glad within, and the breath of the passing breeze is sweet.

From dawn till dusk I sit here before my door, and I know that of a sudden the happy moment will arrive when I shall see.

In the meanwhile I smile and I sing all alone. In the meanwhile the air is filling with the perfume of promise.

光影追逐、风雨相随的夏日，在路边守望是我的快乐。

使者带着未知天空的消息，向我致意后又匆匆赶路。我满心欢喜，吹过的微风也是清甜的。

从清晨到黄昏，我坐在门口，我知道，当我看见你，欢乐的时光便突然降临。

那时，我独自欢笑歌唱。那时，空气中溢满了允诺的芬芳。

45

Have you not heard his silent steps?

He comes, comes, ever comes.

Every moment and every age, every day and every night he comes, comes, ever comes.

Many a song have I sung in many a mood of mind, but all their notes have always proclaimed, "He comes, comes, ever comes."

In the fragrant days of sunny April through the forest path he comes, comes, ever comes.

In the rainy gloom of July nights on the thundering chariot of clouds he comes, comes, ever comes.

In sorrow after sorrow it is his steps that press upon my heart, and it is the golden touch of his feet that makes my joy to shine.

你没听见他静悄悄的脚步吗？

他正走来，走来，不停地走来。

世世代代，朝朝暮暮，时时刻刻，他走来，走来，不停地走来。

在许多不同的心境中，我唱过很多的歌，但所有的音符都宣告："他走来，走来，不停地走来。"

四月芳菲的晴天，他穿过林中的小径走来，走来，不停地走来。

七月阴沉的雨夜，他驾着雷鸣的云车走来，走来，不停地走来。

在悲伤相继中，是他的脚步踏在我心上，正是他的双脚黄金般的触碰，使我的欢乐熠熠生辉。

46

I know not from what distant time thou art ever coming nearer to meet me. Thy sun and stars can never keep thee hidden from me for aye.

In many a morning and eve thy footsteps have been heard and thy messenger has come within my heart and called me in secret.

I know not only why to-day my life is all astir, and a feeling of tremulous joy is passing through my heart.

It is as if the time were come to wind up my work, and I feel in the air a faint smell of thy sweet presence.

我不知道从什么久远的年代，你就一直走近我，来与我相会。太阳和星辰也不能将你永远遮蔽，让我看不见。

朝朝暮暮，我听见你的脚步，你的使者潜入我心中，悄悄地召唤我。

不知道为何，今天我的生命充满骚动，一阵欢欣悸动掠过心头。

就像劳作即将结束的时候，我感到空气中有一股你降临时的清香。

47

The night is nearly spent waiting for him in vain. I fear lest in the morning he suddenly come to my door when I have fallen asleep wearied out. Oh friends, leave the way open to him—forbid him not.

If the sounds of his steps does not wake me, do not try to rouse me, I pray. I wish not to be called from my sleep by the clamorous choir of birds, by the riot of wind at the festival of morning light. Let me sleep undisturbed even if my lord comes of a sudden to my door.

Ah, my sleep, precious sleep, which only waits for his touch to vanish. Ah, my closed eyes that would open their lids only to the light of his smile when he stands before me like a dream emerging from darkness of sleep.

Let him appear before my sight as the first of all lights and all forms. The first thrill of joy to my awakened soul let it come from his glance. And let my return to myself be immediate return to him.

几乎空等了他一整夜。我生怕在清晨筋疲力尽昏昏入睡时，他突然来到我门口。朋友啊，为他让开路——不要阻拦他。

若他的脚步声没有惊醒我，请你们不要唤醒我。我不想被小鸟嘈杂的合唱和风欢庆晨光的呼啸将我从睡梦中唤醒。

就算我的主人突然来到我门口，也不要惊扰我的睡梦。

啊，我的睡眠，珍贵的睡眠，只有他的抚摸能驱散。啊，只有当他站在我面前，像一个梦从沉眠的黑暗中浮现，我紧闭的双眼才会在他微笑的光辉中睁开。

让他作为一切光和形的初始形态出现在我眼前。让我觉醒的灵魂的第一阵欢颤来自他的凝视。让我的自我回归即刻成为对他的皈依。

48

The morning sea of silence broke into ripples of bird songs; and the flowers were all merry by the roadside; and the wealth of gold was scattered through the rift of the clouds while we busily went on our way and paid no heed.

We sang no glad songs nor played; we went not to the village for barter; we spoke not a word nor smiled; we lingered not on the way. We quickened our pave more and more as the time sped by.

The sun rose to the mid sky and doves cooed in the shade. Withered leaves danced and whirled in the hot air of noon. The shepherd boy drowsed and dreamed in the shadow of the banyan tree, and I laid myself down by the water and stretched my tired limbs on the grass.

My companions laughed at me in scorn; they held their heads high and hurried on; they never looked back nor rested; they vanished in the distant blue haze. They crossed many meadows and hills, and passed through strange, far-away countries. All honour to you, heroic host of the interminable path! Mockery and reproach pricked me to rise, but found no response in me. I gave myself up for lost in the depth of a glad humiliation—in the shadow of a dim delight.

The repose of the sun-embroidered green gloom slowly spread over my heart. I forgot for what I had travelled, and I surrendered my mind without struggle to the maze of shadows and songs.

At last, when I woke from my slumber and opened my eyes, I saw thee standing by me, flooding my sleep with thy smile. How I had feared that the path was long and wearisome, and the struggle to reach thee was hard!

清晨宁静的大海泛起鸟儿欢歌的微澜；路边的繁花竞相开放；我们匆匆赶路，无心顾及，云隙里洒下绚烂的金光。

我们既不歌唱，也不游玩；我们没有进村采买；我们一言不发，面无笑容；我们不在路上流连。时间飞逝，我们步伐越来越快。

太阳升到中天，鸽子在阴凉处咕咕叫唤。枯叶在正午的热气中飞舞。牧童在榕树的林荫下沉睡入梦，我躺在水边，在草丛中舒展疲倦的四肢。

我的同伴嘲笑我；他们昂头赶路，既不回望，也不休息，消失在远处的蓝色雾霭中。他们穿过很多草地和山谷，越过陌生遥远的乡村。远征路上的英雄，一切荣耀都属于你们！嘲讽和责备催我起身，但我毫无回应。我自暴自弃，甘愿沉沦在耻辱中——在朦胧的欢乐阴影里。

阳光编织的绿荫的宁静,缓缓铺满我心田。我忘了旅行的目的,不战而降,将心灵交给阴影和欢歌的迷宫。

最后,我从沉睡中醒来,睁开双眼,看见你站在我身边,你的微笑沐浴着我的睡眠。以前我多么担忧,担忧这道路漫长而艰苦,担忧通向你的奋斗历程异常艰难。

49

You came down from your throne and stood at my cottage door.

I was singing all alone in a corner, and the melody caught your ear. You came down and stood at my cottage door.

Masters are many in your hall, and songs are sung there at all hours. But the simple carol of this novice struck at your love. One plaintive little strain mingled with the great music of the world, and with a flower for a prize you came down and stopped at my cottage door.

你走下宝座,站我的草庐门前。

我在屋角独自歌唱,旋律传到你的耳边。你走下来站在我的草庐门前。

你的殿堂里大师云集,歌声不断。这初学者的简单歌曲却得到你的垂爱。一曲忧伤的小调,融入世界的伟大乐章,你带着一朵鲜花作为奖赏,走下宝座驻足在我草庐门前。

50

I had gone a-begging from door to door in the village path, when thy golden chariot appeared in the distance like a gorgeous dream and I wondered who was this King of all kings!

My hopes rose high and me thought my evil days were at an end, and I stood waiting for alms to be given unasked and for wealth scattered on all sides in the dust.

The chariot stopped where I stood. Thy glance fell on me and thou camest down with a smile. I felt that the luck of my life had come at last. Then of a sudden thou didst hold out thy right hand and say "What hast thou to give to me?"

Ah, what a kingly jest was it to open thy palm to a beggar to beg! I was confused and stood undecided, and then from my wallet I slowly took out the least little grain of corn and gave it to thee.

But how great my surprise when at the day's end I emptied my bag on the floor to find a least little gram of gold among the poor heap. I bitterly wept and wished that I had had the heart to give thee my all.

我正在村路上挨户乞讨，你的金辇像一个华美的梦出现在远方，我心想这万王之王是谁！

我的希望高高升起，觉得倒霉日子终于到头了，我站在那里，等待你主动的施舍，还有四散在尘土里的财宝。

车辇停在我站立的地方。你看见我，微笑着下车。我感觉人生的好运终于来临。突然，你伸出右手问我："你有什么可以给我？"

啊，这是什么王者的玩笑，竟然向一个乞丐伸手乞讨！我直犯糊涂，站在那里迟疑不定，然后从我的口袋里慢慢摸出最小的一粒玉米递给你。

但是当一天结束，我把口袋倾空在地，发现在一堆破烂之中有一粒金子时，我是多么震惊。我痛哭流涕，恨不能倾我所有全身心献给你。

51

The night darkened. Our day's works had been done. We thought that the last guest had arrived for the night and the doors in the village were all shut. Only some said the king was to come. We laughed and said "No, it cannot be!"

It seemed there were knocks at the door and we said it was nothing but the wind. We put out the lamps and lay down to sleep. Only some said "It is the messenger!" We laughed and said "No, it must be the wind!"

There came a sound in the dead of the night. We sleepily thought it was the distant thunder. The earth shook, the walls rocked, and it troubled us in our sleep. Only some said it was the sound of wheels. We said in a drowsy murmur, "No, it must be the rumbling of clouds!"

The night was still dark when the drum sounded. The voice came "Wake up! delay not!" We pressed our hands on our hearts and shuddered with fear. Some said, "Lo, there is the king's flag!" We stood up on our feet and cried "There is no time for delay!"

The king has come—but where are lights, where are wreaths? Where is the throne to seat him? Oh, shame! Oh utter shame! Where is the hall, the decorations? Someone has said, "Vain is this cry! Greet him with empty hands, lead him into thy rooms all bare!"

Open the doors, let the conch-shells be sounded! in the depth of the night has come the king of our dark, dreary house. The thunder roars in the sky. The darkness shudders with lightning. Bring out thy tattered piece of mat and spread it in the courtyard. With the storm has come of a sudden our king of the fearful night.

夜已深。我们一天的劳作都已完成。我们以为所有投宿的客人到已到了，村里家家户户都关了门。只是有几个人说国王会降临。我们笑道："不，这不可能！"

似乎有人在敲门，我们说那只是风而已。我们熄灯入睡。只是有人说："那是使者！"我们笑道："不，那一定是风！"

死寂的夜里传来一声巨响。我们在沉睡中以为是远处的雷声。地动墙摇，将我们从睡梦中吵醒。只有几个人说那是车轮的声音。我们困倦地嘟囔："不，肯定是雷鸣！"

鼓声响起时，夜晚依旧漆黑。有人喊道："醒来吧，别耽搁了！"我们用手按住心口，怕得直发抖。有人说："喏，那是国王的旌旗！"我们站起来喊道："没时间再耽搁了！"

国王已经来临——但灯火在哪里，花环在哪里？他的王座在哪里？唉，丢人啊！太丢人了！客厅在哪里？装饰在哪里？有人喊道："哭也没用了！让我们空手迎接他，带他到你一无所有的房间里去！"

　　打开门，吹响螺号吧！在深夜中，国王降临我们黑暗、破旧的房子。雷声在天空激荡。黑暗在闪电中震颤。拿出你破旧的席子铺在院子里。在这恐怖的夜晚，我们的国王与暴风雨一起突然降临。

52

I thought I should ask of thee—but I dared not—the rose wreath thou hadst on thy neck. Thus I waited for the morning, when thou didst depart, to find a few fragments on the bed. And like a beggar I searched in the dawn only for a stray petal or two.

Ah me, what is it I find? What token left of thy love? It is no flower, no spices, no vase of perfumed water. It is thy mighty sword, flashing as a flame, heavy as a bolt of thunder. The young light of morning comes through the window and spread itself upon thy bed. The morning bird twitters and asks, "Woman, what hast thou got?" No, it is no flower, nor spices, nor vase of perfumed water—it is thy dreadful sword.

I sit and muse in wonder, what gift is this of thine. I can find no place to hide it. I am ashamed to wear it, frail as I am, and it hurts me when press it to my bosom. Yet shall I bear in my heart this honour of the burden of pain, this gift of thine.

From now there shall be no fear left for me in this world, and thou shalt be victorious in all my strife. Thou hast left death for my companion and I shall crown him with my life. Thy sword is with me to cut asunder my bonds, and there shall be no fear left for me in the world.

From now I leave off all petty decorations. Lord of my heart, no more shall there be for me waiting and weeping in corners, no more coyness and sweetness of demeanour. Thou hast given me thy sword for adornment. No more doll's decorations for me!

我想向你索求——但又不敢——你颈上的玫瑰花环。就这样等了一早上,当你离开后,在你床上找到一些碎片。拂晓,我像乞丐一样寻觅,只为一两片散落的花瓣。

唉,我找到了什么?你留下了什么爱的信物?不是鲜花,不是香料,也不是一瓶香水。那是你锋利的宝剑,闪如烈焰,重若雷霆。晨光透过窗户,铺洒在你床上。晨鸟叽叽喳喳问道:"姑娘,你得到了什么?"不,不是花朵,不是香料,也不是一瓶香水——是你可畏的宝剑。

我坐下思量,疑惑不解,你这是什么礼物。我无处收藏,也羞于佩带,我如此柔弱,将其拥在胸前会伤到我。但我愿意全心承受你这份礼物,这痛苦负担的荣光。

今后我在这世上无所畏惧,你在我所有战斗中获胜。你让死神与我做伴,我将以生命为其加冕。我用你的宝剑斩断我的枷锁,我在世上无所畏惧。

—吉檀迦利—

今后我将远离一切繁琐的装饰。我心灵的主人，我不会在角落里垂泪等待，也不再娇羞作态。你已将宝剑赠给我佩带。我不再需要玩偶装饰。

53

Beautiful is thy wristlet, decked with stars and cunningly wrought in myriad-coloured jewels. But more beautiful to me thy sword with its curve of lightning like the outspread wings of the divine bird of Vishnu, perfectly poised in the angry red light of the sunset.

It quivers like the one last response of life in ecstasy of pain at the final stroke of death; it shines like the pure flame of being burning up earthly sense with one fierce flash.

Beautiful is thy wristlet, decked with starry gems; but thy sword, O lord of thunder, is wrought with uttermost beauty, terrible to behold or think of.

你的手镯多么精美,装饰着星辰纹饰,精巧地镶着五彩珠宝。但对我而言,更美的是你的宝剑,那闪耀的弧光像毗湿奴的神鸟伸展的翅膀,完美地滑翔在夕阳怒放的红光中。

它震颤着,像在死神最后一击下,生命在痛苦迷离中最后的回响;它闪耀着,像以猛烈的闪光燃尽尘世的精纯烈焰。

你的手镯多么精美,镶着灿若星辰的珠宝;雷霆之主啊,你的宝剑铸得精美绝伦,但让人望而生畏,思之胆战。

54

I asked nothing from thee; I uttered not my name to thine ear. When thou took'st thy leave I stood silent. I was alone by the well where the shadow of the tree fell aslant, and the women had gone home with their brown earthen pitchers full to the brim. They called me and shouted, "Come with us, the morning is wearing on to noon." But I languidly lingered awhile lost in the midst of vague musings.

I heard not thy steps as thou camest. Thine eyes were sad when they fell on me; thy voice was tired as thou spokest low—"Ah, I am a thirsty traveller." I started up from my day-dreams and poured water from my jar on thy joined palms. The leaves rustled overhead; the cuckoo sang from the unseen dark, and perfume of babla flowers came from the bend of the road.

I stood speechless with shame when my name thou didst ask. Indeed, what had I done for thee to keep me in remembrance? But the memory that I could give water to thee to allay thy thirst will cling to my heart and enfold it in sweetness. The morning hour is late, the bird sings in weary notes, neem leaves rustle overhead and I sit and think and think.

我对你一无所求；也不对你说出我的名字。当你离开时我默默站立。我独自站在树影斜垂的井边，姑娘们携着褐色陶罐满载而归。她们呼唤我："跟我们走吧，清晨已过，快到中午了。"但是我仍带着倦意流连，陷入恍惚的沉思中。

我没有听到你走来的脚步声。你看我的目光略带忧伤；你的嗓音疲倦，低声说道："唉，我是疲惫的旅人。"我从梦中惊起，将水从我罐中注入你合拢的手掌。树叶在头顶沙沙作响；布谷鸟在看不见的幽暗中歌唱，曲径上飘来了金合欢的花香。

你问我的名字时，我站在那里羞愧得说不出话。真的，我为你做了什么值得你记住我呢？但我能给你水为你解渴的回忆萦绕在我心头，封存在甜蜜中。天色已晚，鸟儿唱着疲惫的歌，苦楝树叶在头顶沙沙作响，我坐在那里反复思量。

— 吉檀迦利 —

55

Languor is upon your heart and the slumber is still on your eyes.

Has not the word come to you that the flower is reigning in splendour among thorns? Wake, oh awaken! Let not the time pass in vain!

At the end of the stony path, in the country of virgin solitude, my friend is sitting all alone. Deceive him not. Wake, oh awaken!

What if the sky pants and trembles with the heat of the midday sun—what if the burning sand spreads its mantle of thirst—

Is there no joy in the deep of your heart? At every footfall of yours, will not the harp of the road break out in sweet music of pain?

疲倦压在你心上，睡意仍在你眼中。

你还没收到鲜花在荆棘丛中盛开的消息吗？醒来吧，醒来！不要让光阴虚掷！

在石径的尽头，在僻静的荒野，我的朋友独自坐着。不要欺骗他。醒来吧，醒来！

即使正午的骄阳使天空喘息颤抖——即使灼烧的沙漠展开其干渴的斗篷——

你内心深处没有欢乐吗？随着你的每一步，道路的琴弦不会迸出带着痛苦的优美音乐吗？

56

Thus it is that thy joy in me is so full. Thus it is that thou hast come down to me. O thou lord of all heavens, where would be thy love if I were not?

Thou hast taken me as thy partner of all this wealth. In my heart is the endless play of thy delight. In my life thy will is ever taking shape.

And for this, thou who art the King of kings hast decked thyself in beauty to captivate my heart. And for this thy love loses itself in the love of thy lover, and there art thou seen in the perfect union of two.

你的欢乐在我身上如此充盈。你如此俯身迁就我。诸天之主啊，如果没有我，你会爱上谁？

你已将我当作你这一切财富的分享者。你的欢乐在我心中不停地游玩。你的愿望在我生命中不断实现。

因此，你这万王之王装扮自己来俘获我的心。因此，你的爱迷失在你爱人的爱里，在那里，你显现在我们的完美结合中。

57

Light, my light, the world-filling light, the eye-kissing light, heart-sweetening light!

Ah, the light dances, my darling, at the centre of my life; the light strikes, my darling, the chords of my love; the sky opens, the wind runs wild, laughter passes over the earth.

The butterflies spread their sails on the sea of light. Lilies and jasmines surge up on the crest of the waves of light.

The light is shattered into gold on every cloud, my darling, and it scatters gems in profusion.

Mirth spreads from leaf to leaf, my darling, and gladness without measure. The heaven's river has drowned its banks and the flood of joy is abroad.

光，我的光，盈世之光，吻目之光，沁心之光！

啊，亲爱的，光在生命的中心起舞；亲爱的，光拨动我爱的心弦；天开云散，狂风呼啸，欢笑遍地。

蝴蝶在光海上展翅起航；百合和茉莉在光波的浪尖上翻腾。

亲爱的，光在每朵云彩上散落成金，洒下无数珠宝。

亲爱的，快乐在树叶间弥散，欢乐无穷。天河没过了堤岸，欢乐的洪流四处奔涌。

58

Let all the strains of joy mingle in my last song—the joy that makes the earth flow over in the riotous excess of the grass, the joy that sets the twin brothers, life and death, dancing over the wide world, the joy that sweeps in with the tempest, shaking and waking all life with laughter, the joy that sits still with its tears on the open red lotus of pain, and the joy that throws everything it has upon the dust, and knows not a word.

让一切欢乐的旋律都融入我最后的歌中——那使大地在欢腾的草海中涌动的欢乐；那让生与死这对孪生兄弟在浩瀚世界中起舞的欢乐；那和暴风雨一起席卷，用笑声震撼和惊醒一切生灵的欢乐；那含泪静坐在忍痛盛开的红莲上的欢乐；那一无所知，将一切抛掷于尘埃的欢乐。

59

Yes, I know, this is nothing but thy love, O beloved of my heart—this golden light that dances upon the leaves, these idle clouds sailing across the sky, this passing breeze leaving its coolness upon my forehead.

The morning light has flooded my eyes—this is thy message to my heart. Thy face is bent from above, thy eyes look down on my eyes, and my heart has touched thy feet.

是的，我知道，我心爱的人啊，这只是你的爱——这在树叶上起舞的金光，这驶过天空的闲云，这吹过我额头留下清凉的微风。

晨光涌进我双眼——这是你传至我心中的消息。你面容低垂，你的眼睛俯视我的眼睛，而我的心已触及你的双脚。

60

On the seashore of endless worlds children meet. The infinite sky is motionless overhead and the restless water is boisterous. On the seashore of endless worlds the children meet with shouts and dances.

They build their houses with sand and they play with empty shells. With withered leaves they weave their boats and smilingly float them on the vast deep. Children have their play on the seashore of worlds.

They know not how to swim, they know not how to cast nets. Pearl fishers dive for pearls, merchants sail in their ships, while children gather pebbles and scatter them again. They seek not for hidden treasures, they know not how to cast nets.

The sea surges up with laughter and pale gleams the smile of the sea beach. Death-dealing waves sing meaningless ballads to the children, even like a mother while rocking her baby's cradle. The sea plays with children, and pale gleams the smile of the sea beach.

On the seashore of endless worlds children meet. Tempest roams in the pathless sky, ships get wrecked in the trackless water, death is abroad and children play. On the seashore of endless worlds is the great meeting of children.

孩子们相聚在无边世界的海岸。长空无尽高悬其上，波涛不息喧腾于下。孩子们相聚在无边世界的海岸，欢呼起舞。

他们用沙子建造房屋，用空贝壳做游戏。他们把枯叶折成小船，笑着让其漂浮在深广的海上。孩子们在无边世界的海岸嬉戏。

他们不会游泳，也不知道如何撒网。采珠人潜水觅珠，商人们乘船远航，而孩子们只是收集卵石，又随手丢弃。他们不探寻隐秘的宝藏，也不知道如何撒网。

大海涌起笑声，海岸浮现着苍白的微笑。致命的波浪对孩子们唱着无意义的歌谣，就像母亲摇荡着孩子的摇篮。大海与孩子们嬉戏，海岸浮现着苍白的微笑。

孩子们相聚在无边世界的海岸。风暴在无路的天空飘荡，船舶沉没在没有航道的水中，死亡肆虐，孩子们依然在游戏。在无边世界的海岸，是孩子们盛大的聚会。

61

The sleep that flits on baby's eyes—does anybody know from where it comes? Yes, there is a rumour that it has its dwelling where, in the fairy village among shadows of the forest dimly lit with glow-worms, there hang two timid buds of enchantment. From there it comes to kiss baby's eyes.

The smile that flickers on baby's lips when he sleeps—does anybody know where it was born? Yes, there is a rumour that a young pale beam of a crescent moon touched the edge of a vanishing autumn cloud, and there the smile was first born in the dream of a dew-washed morning—the smile that flickers on baby's lips when he sleeps.

The sweet, soft freshness that blooms on baby's limbs—does anybody know where it was hidden so long? Yes, when the mother was a young girl it lay pervading her heart in tender and silent mystery of love—the sweet, soft freshness that has bloomed on baby's limbs.

这掠过婴儿眼睛的睡梦——谁知道它来自哪里?是的,传说它的住所在幽林深处,萤火虫隐约照亮的仙境,那儿挂着两朵含苞欲放的魔法花蕾。睡梦从那儿来亲吻婴儿的眼睛。

这浮现在沉睡的婴儿唇上的微笑——谁知道它源自哪里？是的，传说当新月初绽的清辉触及消散的秋云边缘，微笑便初生在朝露洗净的晨梦中——婴儿沉睡时，这微笑便浮现在他唇上。

这甜蜜柔软的生气洋溢在婴儿的四肢——谁知道它在哪里隐藏那么久？是的，当母亲还是一个少女，它就在温柔宁静的爱的神秘中，弥漫在她心间——这洋溢在婴儿四肢的甜蜜柔软的生气。

62

When I bring to you coloured toys, my child, I understand why there is such a play of colours on clouds, on water, and why flowers are painted in tints—when I give coloured toys to you, my child.

When I sing to make you dance I truly know why there is music in leaves, and why waves send their chorus of voices to the heart of the listening earth—when I sing to make you dance.

When I bring sweet things to your greedy hands I know why there is honey in the cup of the flowers and why fruits are secretly filled with sweet juice—when I bring sweet things to your greedy hands.

When I kiss your face to make you smile, my darling, I surely understand what pleasure streams from the sky in morning light, and what delight that is which the summer breeze brings to my body—when I kiss you to make you smile.

我的孩子，当我带给你多彩的玩具时，我才明白云层和水面为何如此色彩变幻，花朵为何都染上了颜色——当我送你多彩的玩具时，我的孩子。

当我唱歌引你起舞时，我才真正知道绿叶为何生出音乐，波浪为何将合唱送入倾听的大地心中——当我唱歌引你起舞时。

　　当我把甜食递到你渴望的手中时，我才明白花朵的杯盏为何盛满蜜汁，果实为何悄悄贮满了甜浆——当我把甜食递到你渴望的手中时。

　　亲爱的，当我亲吻你的脸蛋逗你欢笑时，我才完全懂得了从天空倾注的晨光中有怎样的欢乐，夏日的微风吹到我身上是何等的惬意——当我亲吻你的脸蛋逗你欢笑时。

63

Thou hast made me known to friends whom I knew not. Thou hast given me seats in homes not my own. Thou hast brought the distant near and made a brother of the stranger.

I am uneasy at heart when I have to leave my accustomed shelter; I forget that there abides the old in the new, and that there also thou abidest.

Through birth and death, in this world or in others, wherever thou leadest me it is thou, the same, the one companion of my endless life who ever linkest my heart with bonds of joy to the unfamiliar.

When one knows thee, then alien there is none, then no door is shut. Oh, grant me my prayer that I may never lose the bliss of the touch of the one in the play of many.

你让素不相识的朋友认识了我。你在别人家里为我留了座位。你化天涯为比邻，使陌路成兄弟。

当我必须辞别故居时，心里惴惴不安；我忘了是旧人迁入新居，而你也住在那里。

走过生与死，在这个世界或别处，不论引领我到哪里都是你，总是你，我无尽生命的唯一伴侣，用欢乐的纽带将我的心与陌生人永远连在一起。

当一个人与你相识,异乡便不再有异客,大门也不再紧闭。啊,请答应我的祈求,让我在与众生的游戏中,永不失去与你单独亲近的幸福。

64

On the slope of the desolate river among tall grasses I asked her, "Maiden, where do you go shading your lamp with your mantle? My house is all dark and lonesome, —lend me your light!" She raised her dark eyes for a moment and looked at my face through the dusk. "I have come to the river," she said, "to float my lamp on the stream when the daylight wanes in the west." I stood alone among tall grasses and watched the timid flame of her lamp uselessly drifting in the tide.

In the silence of gathering night I asked her, "Maiden, your lights are all lit—then where do you go with your lamp? My house is all dark and lonesome, —lend me your light." She raised her dark eyes on my face and stood for a moment doubtful. "I have come," she said at last, "to dedicate my lamp to the sky." I stood and watched her light uselessly burning in the void.

In the moonless gloom of midnight I ask her, "Maiden, what is your quest, holding the lamp near your heart? My house is all dark and lonesome, —lend me your light." She stopped for a minute and thought and gazed at my face in the dark. "I have brought my light," she said, "to join the carnival of lamps." I stood and watched her little lamp uselessly lost among lights.

在荒凉河岸上的深草丛中，我问她："姑娘，你用轻纱罩着灯要去哪里呢？我的房子黑暗孤寂——把你的灯借给我吧！"她缓缓抬起乌黑的眼睛，透过黑暗看着我的脸。她说："当白昼西沉，我来河边把我的灯飘入河中。"我独自站在深草丛中，看着她摇曳的灯光无用地漂荡在细浪中。

在暮色渐浓的寂静中，我问她："姑娘，你的灯全点燃了——你要带着你的灯去哪里？我的房子黑暗孤寂——把你的灯借给我吧！"她抬起乌黑的眼睛看着我的脸，站着迟疑了片刻。最后她说："我来把我的灯献给天空。"我站在那里，看着她的灯在空中无用地燃烧。

在没有月色的幽暗子夜，我问她："姑娘，你把灯捧在心口，在寻找什么？我的房子黑暗孤寂——把你的灯借给我吧！"她驻足沉思片刻，在黑暗中注视着我的脸。她说："我带着我的灯来参加灯会。"我站在那里，看着她小小的灯无用地消失在群灯中。

65

What divine drink wouldst thou have, my God, from this overflowing cup of my life?

My poet, is it thy delight to see thy creation through my eyes and to stand at the portals of my ears silently to listen to thine own eternal harmony?

Thy world is weaving words in my mind and thy joy is adding music to them. Thou givest thyself to me in love and then feelest thine own entire sweetness in me.

我的天帝,你要从我满溢的生命之盏中品饮什么美酒?

我的诗人,透过我的双眼观察你的造物,站在我的耳边静听你永恒的和谐之声,便是你的乐趣吗?

你的世界在我心中编写诗句,你的喜悦又为其配上乐曲。你在爱中将自己献给我,然后在我身上感受你自己圆满的甜美。

66

She who ever had remained in the depth of my being, in the twilight of gleams and of glimpses; she who never opened her veils in the morning light, will be my last gift to thee, my God, folded in my final song.

Words have wooed yet failed to win her; persuasion has stretched to her its eager arms in vain.

I have roamed from country to country keeping her in the core of my heart, and around her have risen and fallen the growth and decay of my life.

Over my thoughts and actions, my slumbers and dreams, she reigned yet dwelled alone and apart.

Many a man knocked at my door and asked for her and turned away in despair.

There was none in the world who ever saw her face to face, and she remained in her loneliness waiting for thy recognition.

在微光闪烁的朦胧中，永远在我生命深处的她，永远不在晨光中揭开面纱的她，将裹在我最后一首歌里，作为我最后送你的礼物，我的天帝。

告白的话语未能赢得她的芳心；劝诱徒劳地向她伸出渴

望的双臂。

我把她藏在心底,四处漫游,我生命的盛衰都围绕着她沉浮。

她主宰我全部的思想和行动、睡眠和梦境,自己却离群索居。

无数人叩响我的门求见她,都失望而去。

世间没有人曾面见其容颜,她仍在孤独中等待你的赏识。

67

Thou art the sky and thou art the nest as well.

O thou beautiful, there in the nest is thy love that encloses the soul with colours and sounds and odours.

There comes the morning with the golden basket in her right hand bearing the wreath of beauty, silently to crown the earth.

And there comes the evening over the lonely meadows deserted by herds, through trackless paths, carrying cool draughts of peace in her golden pitcher from the western ocean of rest.

But there, where spreads the infinite sky for the soul to take her flight in, reigns the stainless white radiance. There is no day nor night, nor form nor colour, and never, never a word.

你是天空，也是巢穴。

啊，美丽的你，巢穴中是你的爱，用色彩、声音、芳香拥簇着灵魂。

清晨在那里降临，右手提着金篮，携着美的花环，悄悄为大地加冕。

黄昏在那里降临，越过被牧群沙化的荒原，穿过踪迹灭绝的幽径，用她的金瓶从宁静的西方海上带来和平的凉气。

但在那里，天空为了灵魂的飞翔而无限延展，充满洁白无瑕的光芒。那里无昼无夜，无形无色，而且永远，永远静寂无言。

68

Thy sunbeam comes upon this earth of mine with arms outstretched and stands at my door the livelong day to carry back to thy feet clouds made of my tears and sighs and songs.

With fond delight thou wrappest about thy starry breast that mantle of misty cloud, turning it into numberless shapes and folds and colouring it with hues everchanging.

It is so light and so fleeting, tender and tearful and dark, that is why thou lovest it, O thou spotless and serene. And that is why it may cover thy awful white light with its pathetic shadows.

你的阳光照临我的大地，整天伸臂站在我门口，把我的眼泪、叹息和歌声化成的云彩带回你脚下。

你怀着喜悦将云雾披风绕在星光闪耀的胸前，变出无数的样式和褶纹，染上变幻无穷的色彩。

它那么轻盈、缥缈，那么纤柔、泪眼盈盈、黯然神伤，因此，圣洁庄严的你才如此怜爱它。这就是为何它能以它楚楚动人的暗影遮蔽你可怖的白光。

69

The same stream of life that runs through my veins night and day runs through the world and dances in rhythmic measures.

It is the same life that shoots in joy through the dust of the earth in numberless blades of grass and breaks into tumultuous waves of leaves and flowers.

It is the same life that is rocked in the ocean-cradle of birth and of death, in ebb and in flow.

I feel my limbs are made glorious by the touch of this world of life. And my pride is from the life-throb of ages dancing in my blood this moment.

同样的生命泉流,在我血管里日夜流动,也流过你的世界,和着音乐的节拍起舞。

是同样的生命,从大地的泥土里欢快地萌发,长出无数草叶,迸发成花与叶的狂潮。

是同样的生命,在潮起潮落中摇荡在生与死的大海摇篮里。

我感到四肢因世界之生命的抚摸而荣耀。我的自豪,源于时代的脉搏此刻在我血管里起舞。

70

Is it beyond thee to be glad with the gladness of this rhythm? To be tossed and lost and broken in the whirl of this fearful joy?

All things rush on, they stop not, they look not behind, no power can hold them back, they rush on.

Keeping steps with that restless, rapid music, seasons come dancing and pass away—colours, tunes, and perfumes pour in endless cascades in the abounding joy that scatters and gives up and dies every moment.

这欢快的节奏不能让你感到快乐吗？不能让你在这可怕的欢乐漩涡中摇荡、迷失和炸裂吗？

万物奔腾，既不停留也不回顾，它们飞奔向前，没有任何力量可以阻挡。

和着飞快不息的音乐节拍，四季蹁跹而来，飘然而去——色彩、旋律、芳香汇成不竭的瀑布倾泻而下，时刻在丰沛的欢乐中飞溅、坠落、消亡。

71

That I should make much of myself and turn it on all sides, thus casting coloured shadows on thy radiance—such is thy maya.

Thou settest a barrier in thine own being and then callest thy severed self in myriad notes. This thy self-separation has taken body in me.

The poignant song is echoed through all the sky in many-coloured tears and smiles, alarms and hopes; waves rise up and sink again, dreams break and form. In me is thy own defeat of self.

This screen that thou hast raised is painted with innumerable figures with the brush of the night and the day. Behind it thy seat is woven in wondrous mysteries of curves, casting away all barren lines of straightness.

The great pageant of thee and me has overspread the sky. With the tune of thee and me all the air is vibrant, and all ages pass with the hiding and seeking of thee and me.

我应该光大自我，传扬四方，将多彩的影子投射在你的光辉中——那是你的幻象。

你在自己体内设置隔断，又以千言万语来呼唤你分隔的自身。你这分隔之身已在我体内成形。

高亢的歌声在诸天回荡，在五彩缤纷的眼泪和微笑、惊恐和希望中应和；潮起潮落，梦灭梦生。在我身上，你击败自我。

　　你卷起的幕帘上，用黑夜和白昼的笔画了无数图案。幕帘后是你的宝座，用奇妙神秘的弧线编织而成，抛弃了所有单调的直线。

　　你我之间的盛会遍布天宇。四周的空气在我们的歌声中震颤，一切时代消逝在你我之间躲藏与寻觅的游戏中。

72

He it is, the innermost one, who awakens my being with his deep hidden touches.

He it is who puts his enchantment upon these eyes and joyfully plays on the chords of my heart in varied cadence of pleasure and pain.

He it is who weaves the web of this maya in evanescent hues of gold and silver, blue and green, and lets peep out through the folds his feet, at whose touch I forget myself.

Days come and ages pass, and it is ever he who moves my heart in many a name, in many a guise, in many a rapture of joy and of sorrow.

就是他,那最神秘的一个,用他深藏的抚摸将我唤醒。

就是他,在我眼中施法,并欢快地在我的心弦上弹出种种悲欢交集的曲调。

就是他,用金银青绿等转瞬即逝的色彩编成幻象之网,从褶皱里露出双脚,在他的触摸下,我忘了自己。

昼夜变换,时代更替,是他永远以诸多名字、诸多化身、诸多大悲和极乐触动我的心。

73

Deliverance is not for me in renunciation. I feel the embrace of freedom in a thousand bonds of delight.

Thou ever pourest for me the fresh draught of thy wine of various colours and fragrance, filling this earthen vessel to the brim.

My world will light its hundred different lamps with thy flame and place them before the altar of thy temple.

No, I will never shut the doors of my senses. The delights of sight and hearing and touch will bear thy delight.

Yes, all my illusions will burn into illumination of joy, and all my desires ripen into fruits of love.

我无须禁欲来寻求解脱。在万千欢愉的束缚中，我感受到自由的拥抱。

你不断往我的陶杯中斟满各种颜色和芳香的新酒。

我的世界将以你的火焰点燃它千百盏各式各样的灯，放在你庙宇的祭坛前。

不，我永不会关闭我的感观之门。色、声、触的欢乐会承载你的欢乐。

是的，我的一切幻想将燃烧成欢乐的光明，我的所有欲望将圆熟成爱的果实。

74

The day is no more, the shadow is upon the earth. It is time that I go to the stream to fill my pitcher.

The evening air is eager with the sad music of the water. Ah, it calls me out into the dusk. In the lonely lane there is no passer-by, the wind is up, the ripples are rampant in the river.

I know not if I shall come back home. I know not whom I shall chance to meet. There at the fording in the little boat the unknown man plays upon his lute.

白昼已尽,暗影笼罩大地。我该去河边汲满我的水罐了。

夜晚的空气在流水的哀歌中充满期盼。唉,它召唤我走进暮色中。荒凉的小路上杳无人迹,风乍起,河面水波荡漾。

我不知是否应该回家。我不知会偶遇谁。渡口的小舟里,有个陌生人在弹着他的鲁特琴。

75

Thy gifts to us mortals fulfil all our needs and yet run back to thee undiminished.

The river has its everyday work to do and hastens through fields and hamlets; yet its incessant stream winds towards the washing of thy feet.

The flower sweetens the air with its perfume; yet its last service is to offer itself to thee.

Thy worship does not impoverish the world.

From the words of the poet men take what meanings please them; yet their last meaning points to thee.

你的馈赠满足了我们芸芸众生的一切需求，又分毫不减地回到你那里。

溪流每天肩负职责，匆匆穿过田野和乡村，那不息的清流又转回去濯洗你的双足。

花朵的芬香弥漫在空中，但它最终的使命，是将自己献给你。

敬拜你不会使世界贫瘠。

人们从诗人的字句中选取自己喜欢的意义，但它们的终极意义都指向你。

76

Day after day, O lord of my life, shall I stand before thee face to face. With folded hands, O lord of all worlds, shall I stand before thee face to face.

Under thy great sky in solitude and silence, with humble heart shall I stand before thee face to face.

In this laborious world of thine, tumultuous with toil and with struggle, among hurrying crowds shall I stand before thee face to face.

And when my work shall be done in this world, O King of kings, alone and speechless shall I stand before thee face to face.

日复一日，啊，我的生命之主，我能否与你面对面站立？啊，大千世界之主，我能否双手合十与你面对面站立？

在你浩瀚孤寂的苍穹下，我能否怀着谦卑之心与你面对面站立？

在你辛劳的世界里，喧嚣着劳作和挣扎，在熙攘的人群中，我能否与你面对面站立？

啊，万王之王，当我完成此生的工作，孤独无言，我能否与你面对面站立？

77

I know thee as my God and stand apart—I do not know thee as my own and come closer. I know thee as my father and bow before thy feet—I do not grasp thy hand as my friend's.

I stand not where thou comest down and ownest thyself as mine, there to clasp thee to my heart and take thee as my comrade.

Thou art the Brother amongst my brothers, but I heed them not, I divide not my earnings with them, thus sharing my all with thee.

In pleasure and in pain I stand not by the side of men, and thus stand by thee. I shrink to give up my life, and thus do not plunge into the great waters of life.

我视你为我的天帝并敬而远之——我不知道你属于我并亲近你。我视你为父并拜倒在你脚边——我没有像朋友一样紧握你的手。

我没有站在你降临之处把你当成我的,没有把你拥在怀里并把你当作我的同伴。

你是我所有兄弟中的兄长,但我不理睬他们,不与他们分享我的收入,以为这样就能与你分享一切。

在欢乐与痛苦中，我没有站在众生一边，以为这样就能站在你身边。我畏缩不前，不敢舍弃生命，因此没有跳入生命的汪洋。

吉檀迦利

78

When the creation was new and all the stars shone in their first splendour, the gods held their assembly in the sky and sang "Oh, the picture of perfection! the joy unalloyed!"

But one cried of a sudden —"It seems that somewhere there is a break in the chain of light and one of the stars has been lost."

The golden string of their harp snapped, their song stopped, and they cried in dismay —"Yes, that lost star was the best, she was the glory of all heavens!"

From that day the search is unceasing for her, and the cry goes on from one to the other that in her the world has lost its one joy!

Only in the deepest silence of night the stars smile and whisper among themselves —"Vain is this seeking! Unbroken perfection is over all!"

创世之初，群星初绽光芒，众神聚集在天宫歌唱："啊，完美的图景！纯粹的欢乐！"

忽然，一位天神叫道："光链上似乎有个缺口，一颗星走失了。"

竖琴金弦崩裂，歌声戛然而止，众神失声叫道："是啊，失去的星星是最好的，她是诸天的荣耀。"

此后，他们不停地寻觅她，奔走呼号，都说世界因为失去她而失去了一份欢乐！

只有在最深沉的静夜里，群星微笑着窃窃私语："寻找只是徒劳！完美无缺笼罩着一切！"

If it is not my portion to meet thee in this life then let me ever feel that I have missed thy sight—let me not forget for a moment, let me carry the pangs of this sorrow in my dreams and in my wakeful hours.

As my days pass in the crowded market of this world and my hands grow full with the daily profits, let me ever feel that I have gained nothing—let me not forget for a moment, let me carry the pangs of this sorrow in my dreams and in my wakeful hours.

When I sit by the roadside, tired and panting, when I spread my bed low in the dust, let me ever feel that the long journey is still before me—let me not forget a moment, let me carry the pangs of this sorrow in my dreams and in my wakeful hours.

When my rooms have been decked out and the flutes sound and the laughter there is loud, let me ever feel that I have not invited thee to my house—let me not forget for a moment, let me carry the pangs of this sorrow in my dreams and in my wakeful hours.

如果今生无缘遇见你，就让我永远感受错过你的目光——让我片刻不忘，带着这遗憾的痛苦，不论梦中还是清醒。

随着日子在世界的闹市里流逝，我双手捧满每日的盈利，让我永远感觉一无所获——让我片刻不忘，带着这遗憾的痛苦，不论梦中还是清醒。

当我坐在路边，疲惫喘息，我在尘土里铺开铺盖，让我永远感觉前路依然漫长——让我片刻不忘，带着这遗憾的痛苦，不论梦中还是清醒。

当我将房间装饰一新，笛声和欢笑传来，让我永远感到不曾邀你光临寒舍——让我片刻不忘，带着这遗憾的痛苦，不论梦中还是清醒。

80

I am like a remnant of a cloud of autumn uselessly roaming in the sky, O my sun ever-glorious! Thy touch has not yet melted my vapour, making me one with thy light, and thus I count months and years separated from thee.

If this be thy wish and if this be thy play, then take this fleeting emptiness of mine, paint it with colours, gild it with gold, float it on the wanton wind and spread it in varied wonders.

And again when it shall be thy wish to end this play at night, I shall melt and vanish away in the dark, or it may be in a smile of the white morning, in a coolness of purity transparent.

我像一片秋天的残云,徒劳地在天空飘荡,啊,我永远光辉的太阳!你的触碰没有融化我的水汽,使我与你的光明合一,因此我细数着与你分离的岁月。

如果这就是你的意愿,这就是你的游戏,请拿走我流逝的空虚,染上颜色,镀上金光,让它漂浮在无常的风中,舒卷成各种奇观。

如你愿意在夜晚结束这场游戏,我愿消融在黑暗中,在晨光的微笑中,或在纯净的清凉中。

81

On many an idle day have I grieved over lost time. But it is never lost, my lord. Thou hast taken every moment of my life in thine own hands.

Hidden in the heart of things thou art nourishing seeds into sprouts, buds into blossoms, and ripening flowers into fruitfulness.

I was tired and sleeping on my idle bed and imagined all work had ceased. In the morning I woke up and found my garden full with wonders of flowers.

在那些闲散的日子，我痛惜时光的流逝。但光阴从未虚掷，我的主人。你掌握着我生命的每一寸光阴。

你藏在万物心中，滋养着种子萌发，花蕾盛开，繁花结出硕果。

我累了，在闲榻上睡去，想象着一切劳作都已完成。清晨醒来，却发现我的园中遍开奇花。

82

Time is endless in thy hands, my lord. There is none to count thy minutes.

Days and nights pass and ages bloom and fade like flowers. Thou knowest how to wait.

Thy centuries follow each other perfecting a small wild flower.

We have no time to lose, and having no time we must scramble for a chances. We are too poor to be late.

And thus it is that time goes by while I give it to every querulous man who claims it, and thine altar is empty of all offerings to the last.

At the end of the day I hasten in fear lest thy gate to be shut; but I find that yet there is time.

我的主人，你手里的时间无穷无尽。你的分分秒秒无法计算。

昼夜更替，时代兴衰如花开花落。你知道如何等待。

你接连不断花费数个世纪只为完善一朵微小的野花。

我们没有时间可浪费，必须争分夺秒抓住机会。我们太穷困了，耽搁不起。

当我把时间让给每一个匆匆向我索取的人，时间就那样流逝了，最终你的祭坛上没有一点祭品。

一天将尽，我匆忙赶来，唯恐你的大门关闭；但我发现时间还很充裕。

83

Mother, I shall weave a chain of pearls for thy neck with my tears of sorrow.

The stars have wrought their anklets of light to deck thy feet, but mine will hang upon thy breast.

Wealth and fame come from thee and it is for thee to give or to withhold them. But this my sorrow is absolutely mine own, and when I bring it to thee as my offering thou rewardest me with thy grace.

圣母，我要用我悲伤的泪水编一条珠链挂在你颈上。

繁星将光芒铸成脚镯装饰你的双足，但我的珠链要挂在你胸前。

财富和名声都源于你，全凭你赐予或剥夺。但我这悲伤完全是自己的，当我将其作为祭品献给你时，你用你的慈悲酬谢我。

84

It is the pang of separation that spreads throughout the world and gives birth to shapes innumerable in the infinite sky.

It is this sorrow of separation that gazes in silence all nights from star to star and becomes lyric among rustling leaves in rainy darkness of July.

It is this overspreading pain that deepens into loves and desires, into sufferings and joy in human homes; and this it is that ever melts and flows in songs through my poet's heart.

离愁弥漫世界,在无尽的苍穹生出无数景象。

正是这离愁整夜静静地凝望群星,在七月阴雨中萧萧的树叶间化作抒情的诗篇。

正是这弥漫的痛苦深入爱和欲望,深入人世间的苦难和欢乐;正是它通过我的诗人之心,不断融化、流淌成歌。

85

When the warriors came out first from their master's hall, where had they hid their power? Where were their armour and their arms?

They looked poor and helpless, and the arrows were showered upon them on the day they came out from their master's hall.

When the warriors marched back again to their master's hall where did they hide their power?

They had dropped the sword and dropped the bow and the arrow; peace was on their foreheads, and they had left the fruits of their life behind them on the day they marched back again to their master's hall.

当战士们第一次走出将领的大堂,他们的武力藏在哪里?他们的盔甲和武器在哪里?

他们看起来可怜无助,他们走出将领的大堂那天,箭矢如雨射向他们。

当战士们列队返回将领的大堂,他们的武力藏在哪里?

他们放下刀剑,抛下弓矢;和平在他们额头闪现,他们列队返回将领的大堂那天,已将人生的果实留在身后。

86

Death, thy servant, is at my door. He has crossed the unknown sea and brought thy call to my home.

The night is dark and my heart is fearful—yet I will take up the lamp, open my gates and bow to him my welcome. It is thy messenger who stands at my door.

I will worship him with folded hands, and with tears. I will worship him placing at his feet the treasure of my heart.

He will go back with his errand done, leaving a dark shadow on my morning; and in my desolate home only my forlorn self will remain as my last offering to thee.

死神，你的仆人，正在我门口。他渡过未知的海，把你的召唤带到我家。

夜色深沉，我心惶恐——但我仍提起灯，打开门，鞠躬欢迎他。因为站在我门口的是你的信使。

我要敬拜他，双手合十，眼含泪水。我要敬拜他，把心中的珍宝放在他脚下。

他将回去复命，在我的清晨中留下一个暗影；我空荡的家中，只剩下我孤身一人，作为我最后的祭品献给你。

87

In desperate hope I go and search for her in all the corners of my room; I find her not.

My house is small and what once has gone from it can never be regained.

But infinite is thy mansion, my lord, and seeking her I have to come to thy door.

I stand under the golden canopy of thine evening sky and I lift my eager eyes to thy face.

I have come to the brink of eternity from which nothing can vanish—no hope, no happiness, no vision of a face seen through tears.

Oh, dip my emptied life into that ocean, plunge it into the deepest fullness. Let me for once feel that lost sweet touch in the allness of the universe.

在无望的希望中，我走遍房间的每个角落寻找她，但没有找到。

我的房间狭小，一旦丢失什么就再也找不到。

但你的殿堂无边无际，我的主人，为寻找她，我来到你的门前。

我站在你夜空里金色的穹顶下，抬起渴望的双眼，仰望着你的脸。

我来到永恒的边界，在这里，万物不灭——不论希望，幸福，还是透过泪光看到的容颜。

啊，将我空虚的人生浸入那片汪洋，投入最深的圆满中。让我在宇宙的完满中，再次感受那失去的甜美爱抚。

88

Deity of the ruined temple! The broken strings of Vina sing no more your praise. The bells in the evening proclaim not your time of worship. The air is still and silent about you.

In your desolate dwelling comes the vagrant spring breeze. It brings the tidings of flowers—the flowers that for your worship are offered no more.

Your worshipper of old wanders ever longing for favour still refused. In the eventide, when fires and shadows mingle with the gloom of dust, he wearily comes back to the ruined temple with hunger in his heart.

Many a festival day comes to you in silence, deity of the ruined temple. Many a night of worship goes away with lamp unlit.

Many new images are built by masters of cunning art and carried to the holy stream of oblivion when their time is come.

Only the deity of the ruined temple remains unworshipped in deathless neglect.

破庙里的神啊!七弦琴的断弦不再弹奏你的赞歌。晚钟也不再宣告祭拜你的时辰。你周围的空气凝重而沉寂。

飘荡的春风吹进你荒寂的居所。它来带了花的消息——

已无人敬献祭拜你的鲜花。

你往日那漂泊的祭拜者,总在期盼那未曾允诺的恩典。黄昏时分,烛火与暗影交织在尘土的幽暗中,他疲惫地返回破庙,心中满怀渴望。

破庙里的神啊,无数佳节在冷寂中降临。无数祭拜的夜晚,在没有灯火的黑暗中流逝。

许多新的神像被能工巧匠制作出来,时间一到,便被抛入遗忘的圣泉。

唯有破庙里的神,残留在无尽的漠视里,无人祭拜。

89

No more noisy, loud words from me—such is my master's will. Henceforth I deal in whispers. The speech of my heart will be carried on in murmurings of a song.

Men hasten to the King's market. All the buyers and sellers are there. But I have my untimely leave in the middle of the day, in the thick of work.

Let then the flowers come out in my garden, though it is not their time; and let the midday bees strike up their lazy hum.

Full many an hour have I spent in the strife of the good and the evil, but now it is the pleasure of my playmate of the empty days to draw my heart on to him; and I know not why is this sudden call to what useless inconsequence!

我不再喧闹,不再高谈阔论——这是主人的意愿。从此我轻声细语。我将用一曲轻歌唱出心中的话语。

人们匆匆赶往国王的集市。买卖的人都聚集在那里。但这繁忙的正午,我提前离开了。

就让鲜花在我的园中盛放,虽然花期未至;让晌午的蜜蜂慵懒地振翅嗡鸣。

我花费了太多时间在善恶之间挣扎，但现在这闲暇日子，本该由玩伴兴致勃勃地地将我的心带到他那儿去；但我不知道为什么，又突然唤起什么无益的矛盾！

90

On the day when death will knock at thy door what wilt thou offer to him?

Oh, I will set before my guest the full vessel of my life—I will never let him go with empty hands.

All the sweet vintage of all my autumn days and summer nights, all the earnings and gleanings of my busy life will I place before him at the close of my days when death will knock at my door.

死神来叩门那天,你以什么敬献他?

啊,我将在客人面前摆上我满斟的生命之盏——我决不让他空手而归。

在我生命尽头,当死神来叩门,我秋日和夏夜酿制的所有美酒,我劳碌一生的所有收获和珍藏,都将摆在他面前。

91

O thou the last fulfilment of life, Death, my death, come and whisper to me!

Day after day I have kept watch for thee; for thee have I borne the joys and pangs of life.

All that I am, that I have, that I hope and all my love have ever flowed towards thee in depth of secrecy. One final glance from thine eyes and my life will be ever thine own.

The flowers have been woven and the garland is ready for the bridegroom. After the wedding the bride shall leave her home and meet her lord alone in the solitude of night.

啊，你这生命最后的圆满，死亡，我的死亡，来吧，对我低语。

我天天守望着你；为你承受生命的悲欢。

我的一切存在，一切拥有，一切希望，一切爱，都在秘密深处流向你。你的眼睛向我最后一瞥，我的生命便永归于你。

为新郎准备的花环已编好。婚礼之后，新娘就要离家，在静夜独自面对她的主人。

92

I know that the day will come when my sight of this earth shall be lost, and life will take its leave in silence, drawing the last curtain over my eyes.

Yet stars will watch at night, and morning rise as before, and hours heave like sea waves casting up pleasures and pains.

When I think of this end of my moments, the barrier of the moments breaks and I see by the light of death thy world with its careless treasures. Rare is its lowliest seat, rare is its meanest of lives.

Things that I longed for in vain and things that I got—let them pass. Let me but truly possess the things that I ever spurned and overlooked.

我知道这一天即将来临，尘世将从我眼前消逝，生命悄然辞别，拉过最后的帷幕遮住我双眼。

星辰仍在夜间凝望，黎明照常升起，时光汹涌如海浪，激荡着悲欢。

当我想到我岁月的终点，时光的栅栏裂开，在死亡之光中，我看见你散落着珍宝的世界。它最卑微的座位多么珍稀，它最卑贱的生灵多么高贵。

我求而不得和已经获得的东西——都让它们消逝吧。只让我真正拥有那些我一直抛弃和忽视的东西。

——吉檀迦利

93

I have got my leave. Bid me farewell, my brothers! I bow to you all and take my departure.

Here I give back the keys of my door—and I give up all claims to my house. I only ask for last kind words from you.

We were neighbours for long, but I received more than I could give. Now the day has dawned and the lamp that lit my dark corner is out. A summons has come and I am ready for my journey.

我已经获准离去。祝福我吧,兄弟们!我向你们鞠躬告别。

在此我归还房门的钥匙——我放弃对房子的所有权利。我只请求你们最后的美言。

我们长久为邻,但我的获取远多于付出。现在天已破晓,照亮我昏暗屋角的灯已熄灭。召唤已至,我准备启程了。

94

At this time of my parting, wish me good luck, my friends! The sky is flushed with the dawn and my path lies beautiful.

Ask not what I have with me to take there. I start on my journey with empty hands and expectant heart.

I shall put on my wedding garland. Mine is not the red-brown dress of the traveller, and though there are dangers on the way I have no fear in mind.

The evening star will come out when my voyage is done and the plaintive notes of the twilight melodies be struck up from the King's gateway.

在我离别的时刻，祝我好运吧，朋友！天空泛着晨光，我的前路美好。

不要问我带些什么过去。我只带着空空的双手和期待的心出发。

我要戴上婚礼的花环。我没有穿红褐色的旅行衣，虽然路途艰险，但我心无畏惧。

在我的旅途尽头，夜空中星星升起，王宫门口响起黄昏的哀乐。

95

I was not aware of the moment when I first crossed the threshold of this life.

What was the power that made me open out into this vast mystery like a bud in the forest at midnight!

When in the morning I looked upon the light I felt in a moment that I was no stranger in this world, that the inscrutable without name and form had taken me in its arms in the form of my own mother.

Even so, in death the same unknown will appear as ever known to me. And because I love this life, I know I shall love death as well.

The child cries out when from the right breast the mother takes it away, in the very next moment to find in the left one its consolation.

我对初次跨过此生门槛的那一瞬间毫无知觉。

究竟是什么力量使我在浩瀚的神秘中开放,就像一朵花蕾子夜时分在林中绽放。

清晨,我抬头看到天光,立刻感到我并不是这个世界的生人,那无名无形不可思议者,以母亲的形象将我拥在臂弯。

尽管如此，在死亡中这同一个不可知者仍会以我熟识的面容出现。因为我热爱此生，我知道我会同样热爱死亡。

当母亲把婴儿从右乳移开，孩子哭喊着，立刻又在左乳找到了安慰。

96

When I go from hence let this be my parting word, that what I have seen is unsurpassable.

I have tasted of the hidden honey of this lotus that expands on the ocean of light, and thus am I blessed—let this be my parting word.

In this playhouse of infinite forms I have had my play and here have I caught sight of him that is formless.

My whole body and my limbs have thrilled with his touch who is beyond touch; and if the end comes here, let it come—let this be my parting word.

当我离开这里,就让我如此话别:我所见过的无与伦比。

我尝过盛开在光海中的莲花里隐藏的花蜜,并因此受到祝福——就让我如此话别。

在这形象无穷的乐园,我已纵情游玩,并窥见过无形的他。

他遥不可及,我的身躯和四肢却因他的触摸而战栗;若大限将至,就让它来吧——就让我如此话别。

97

When my play was with thee I never questioned who thou wert. I knew nor shyness nor fear, my life was boisterous.

In the early morning thou wouldst call me from my sleep like my own comrade and lead me running from glade to glade.

On those days I never cared to know the meaning of songs thou sangest to me. Only my voice took up the tunes, and my heart danced in their cadence.

Now, when the playtime is over, what is this sudden sight that is come upon me? The world with eyes bent upon thy feet stands in awe with all its silent stars.

当我与你游戏时,我从未问过你是谁。我既不羞怯,也不畏惧,我的生活欢快热闹。

清晨,你像我的玩伴一样,将我从睡梦中唤醒,领着我在旷野中奔跑。

那些日子,我从不想去了解你对我所唱歌曲的意义。只是我的声音和着你的旋律,我的心随着节拍起舞。

现在,游戏时光结束,这突然出现在我面前的景象是什么?世界俯视着你的双脚,携其静穆的群星恭敬地站立。

98

I will deck thee with trophies, garlands of my defeat. It is never in my power to escape unconquered.

I surely know my pride will go to the wall, my life will burst its bonds in exceeding pain, and my empty heart will sob out in music like a hollow reed, and the stone will melt in tears.

I surely know the hundred petals of a lotus will not remain closed for ever and the secret recess of its honey will be bared.

From the blue sky an eye shall gaze upon me and summon me in silence. Nothing will be left for me, nothing whatever, and utter death shall I receive at thy feet.

我将以我失败的花环作为战利品来装饰你。我永远无力逃脱你的征服。

我确知我的骄傲会碰壁，我的生命将在极度的痛苦中冲决束缚，我空虚的心如一支空苇呜咽出哀歌，顽石也将在泪水中融化。

我确知莲花的百瓣不会永远闭合，其隐藏的花蜜终将显露。

有一只眼睛从碧空中默默注视并召唤我。我将失去一切，彻底一无所有，在你脚下领受终极的死亡。

99

When I give up the helm I know that the time has come for thee to take it. What there is to do will be instantly done. Vain is this struggle.

Then take away your hands and silently put up with your defeat, my heart, and think it your good fortune to sit perfectly still where you are placed.

These my lamps are blown out at every little puff of wind, and trying to light them I forget all else again and again.

But I shall be wise this time and wait in the dark, spreading my mat on the floor; and whenever it is thy pleasure, my lord, come silently and take thy seat here.

当我放开舵盘，便知道由你接管的时候到了。该做之事应立即做完，挣扎只是徒劳。

那就放开你的手，默默承认你的失败吧，我的心，要想到你能安坐在你的位置，已经是你的幸运了。

我这些灯被一阵又一阵微风吹灭，为了点燃它们，我一再忘了所有其余的事。

这次我要聪明点，把我的席子铺在地上，在黑暗中等待；我的主人，什么时候你高兴，就悄悄过来坐在这里。

100

I dive down into the depth of the ocean of forms, hoping to gain the perfect pearl of the formless.

No more sailing from harbour to harbour with this my weather-beaten boat. The days are long passed when my sport was to be tossed on waves.

And now I am eager to die into the deathless.

Into the audience hall by the fathomless abyss where swells up the music of toneless strings I shall take this harp of my life.

I shall tune it to the notes of forever, and when it has sobbed out its last utterance, lay down my silent harp at the feet of the silent.

我潜入形象之海的深处，希望获取无形的完美珍珠。

我不再驾驶这饱经风雨的旧船穿梭于各个海港，我弄潮搏浪的岁月早已远去。

此刻，我渴望死于不死之中。

我要拿起我这生命的竖琴，进入无底深渊旁那飘荡着单调弦乐的殿堂。

我调理琴弦，和着那永恒的音调，当其呜咽完最后的余音，我便将静默的竖琴放在宁静的脚边。

101

Ever in my life have I sought thee with my songs. It was they who led me from door to door, and with them have I felt about me, searching and touching my world.

It was my songs that taught me all the lessons I ever learnt; they showed me secret paths, they brought before my sight many a star on the horizon of my heart.

They guided me all the day long to the mysteries of the country of pleasure and pain, and, at last, to what palace gate have the brought me in the evening at the end of my journey?

终我一生,我以诗歌来追寻你。是它们领我穿过一扇又一扇门,靠它们我才感知到自己,探索和接触我的世界。

我的诗歌教会我所学的一切功课,为我指明隐秘的道路,把我心中地平线上的星辰带到我眼前。

它们整天领着我走进快乐和痛苦的神秘国度,最后,在我旅程结束的黄昏,它们会把我带到哪座宫殿的门口?

102

I boasted among men that I had known you. They see your pictures in all works of mine. They come and ask me, "Who is he?" I know not how to answer them. I say, "Indeed, I cannot tell." They blame me and they go away in scorn. And you sit there smiling.

I put my tales of you into lasting songs. The secret gushes out from my heart. They come and ask me, "Tell me all your meanings." I know not how to answer them. I say, "Ah, who knows what they mean!" They smile and go away in utter scorn. And you sit there smiling.

我向众人夸耀说我认识你。他们在我所有作品里看到你的画像。他们过来问我："他是谁？"我不知如何回答。我说："其实，我说不上来。"他们责怪我，轻蔑地走了。而你坐在那里微笑。

我把你的传奇编成不朽的歌。秘密从我心中涌出。他们过来问我："把所有意义告诉我们吧。"我不知如何回答。我说："唉，谁知道那是什么意思！"他们冷笑着，极其鄙夷地走了。而你坐在那里微笑。

103

In one salutation to thee, my God, let all my senses spread out and touch this world at thy feet.

Like a rain-cloud of July hung low with its burden of unshed showers let all my mind bend down at thy door in one salutation to thee.

Let all my songs gather together their diverse strains into a single current and flow to a sea of silence in one salutation to thee.

Like a flock of homesick cranes flying night and day back to their mountain nests let all my life take its voyage to its eternal home in one salutation to thee.

在对你的敬拜中,我的天帝,让我所有的感官舒展,触及你脚下的世界。

在对你的敬拜中,让我全心俯首在你门口,如七月的积雨云背负着雨水低垂。

在对你的敬拜中,让我所有的歌曲将不同的曲调汇成一股洪流,流向宁静的大海。

在对你的敬拜中,让我全部的生命向永恒的家园出发,如一群思乡的鹤,日夜不停飞向它们的山中的归巢。